P9-CQI-786

STEALING AIR

TRENT REEDY

STEALING AIR

ARTHUR A. LEVINE BOOKS

An imprint of Scholastic Inc.

Library of Congress Cataloging-in-Publication Data
Reedy, Trent.
Stealing air / Trent Reedy. — 1st ed.
p. cm.
Summary: Three sixth-grade boys band together to build an experimental aircraft, enduring social and practical difficulties in the process.
ISBN 978-0-545-38307-3 (hardcover : alk. paper)
[1. Inventions — Fiction. 2. Airplanes — Fiction.
3. Friendship — Fiction.] I. Title.
PZ7.R25423St 2012
[Fic] — dc23
2011046290

10 9 8 7 6 5 4 3 2 1   12 13 14 15 16
Printed in the U.S.A.   23
First edition, October 2012

Always for Amanda.

"Great success through great risk," Brian whispered as he jumped his skateboard off the curb. There were over a dozen kids carving tricks at the skate park just ahead of him. Brian didn't know any of them, but since tomorrow would be his first day at a new school, he might as well do something to start making friends. He stomped the tail of his skateboard to ollie it onto the next sidewalk.

This was his fourth day in Riverside, Iowa, but the first time he had been allowed to do much of anything besides carry things into the new house, unpack, and clean. He was glad to see that a lot of these kids looked like they could be heading into the sixth grade like he was. Most had skateboards. Some were Rollerblading. One girl jumped the ramps on her bike. A group of guys was skating the half-pipe, trying to complete a whole run down one six-foot ramp, up the other, and back again. So far, he hadn't seen anyone make it.

Brian rolled up closer as one skater put his back truck over the lip of the ramp, standing on the tail to keep the board on the deck. He stared down the ramp, breathing heavy. Brian shook his head. The kid was skater spooked. He had waited too long and thought about the trick too much. When he finally dropped into the curve, he lost his balance right away. The board wobbled and flew out from under him, and he went rolling down to the flat bottom.

Another kid moved to the edge, pushing some of the others back. "Out of the way! Give me room!" He was short and compact, but he had rolled up the sleeves on his plain black T-shirt, showing off his biceps. "I can do it! I almost did it yesterday," he said. He pushed his curly black hair out of his eyes. "This time I'll do the whole run."

"Five bucks says you can't do it, Frankie," said a guy with short-cropped blond hair. "Up the other side and back without falling."

"You're on, Alex," said Frankie. "You better have the money."

"I always have money," said Alex.

Frankie positioned his skateboard on the lip of the ramp, front wheels up. He took a breath and then dropped into the transition. His lean was good. His board was steady. Brian figured he might make it. Up the other transition to the far side. Would he kickturn or just tap off the lip and ride back down fakie? He went for the kickturn, a pretty good one. But he messed up the transition going down and came in unbalanced. His board went rolling away from him just as he approached the other transition, and he landed on his butt.

The guys up on the deck clapped. Some groaned, saying he'd been so close. Alex just smiled. Frankie punched the ground and got up to go after his board. It had rolled over by Brian, so Brian picked it up and held it out to him. "Good skating," he said. "Next time, when you're —"

"Shut up!" Frankie yanked his skateboard out of Brian's grip. "I'm the best skater in town. I don't need tips from freaks like you." He went back to the half-pipe. "This guy here . . ." He jerked a thumb in Brian's direction as he climbed the stairs up to the deck. "This guy is trying to give *me* tips on skating."

Some of the others laughed. Brian felt his cheeks go hot and hoped he wasn't too red. This move to Riverside was supposed to be a chance to start fresh. If he was going to make any friends, he needed to make a move now. Take the big risk.

"I bet I can do it," he called up to the guys. He picked up his board by the front truck and made his way up the steps. Dad always said the best way to make friends was just to jump in and talk to people as though they already were your friends. Nobody seemed to notice him now, though. As Frankie handed his five-dollar bill to Alex, Brian swallowed and spoke louder. "I bet I can do it."

Heads turned toward him. Alex raised his eyebrows. Frankie moved back and put his hands on his hips. "I'd like to see you try."

Alex shook his recent winnings in the air. "Five bucks?"

Brian shrugged. "Make it ten." He had to carve this trick right to shut Frankie up and impress the others. Plus, he didn't have ten bucks.

Alex laughed and typed something on the iPhone that he took out of his pocket. "All right, dude. You're on."

Brian put his wheels over the lip with the tail of the board still on the deck. His hands were sweaty and his stomach felt hollow. He had to move fast to avoid skater spook. He stomped hard on the front of his skateboard, *Spitfire*, and leaned forward into the drop.

Into the first curve like a free fall, smooth and tight, zipping across the flat at the bottom. He bent his legs as he shot up the other transition. Grinding his trucks on the lip, he kicked it around and leaned into the drop. He rolled over the flat and up the other side to park it right on the lip with his front wheels up. Leaning forward, he let his board hit the deck and let out a shaky breath.

Everyone shouted and clapped. A skater with bright red hair yelled, "Awesome!"

"I have *never* seen moves like that on this ramp," another kid said.

Brian grinned. Maybe Dad had been right. Maybe all he needed to do was take a risk. Alex shook his head and took a five from his wallet, which he handed over with Frankie's money.

"Can you get air?" One of the skaters took off her purple helmet and ran her hand through long black hair. When Brian saw her smile and her bright green eyes, he froze. This girl was an angel. The angel laughed a little. "Well, can you?"

"Um." Brian swallowed. "What?"

"She asked if you can get air! You deaf?" Frankie shouted.

This guy was starting to be a major pain. Brian knew he had to go for it. He had scored air on the half-pipe back in Seattle a bunch of times, but he was still trying to pull off the Ultimate Trick, a full 360-degree spin in the air at the top of the ramp. He could do a simple jump now, though. He set *Spitfire* up for the drop into the half-pipe, and people cheered.

Frankie leaned against the railing at the back of the deck. "No way. He's gonna get hurt."

"Five bucks says he can do it!" the angel shouted.

Alex whipped out his iPhone again and started typing. "Wendy bets five. Any takers?"

"You nuts?" said Frankie. "Ten says he can't get off the ground."

Others chimed in with their bets. Alex keyed it all into his phone. He gave Brian the thumbs-up. "Okay, dude. Go for it."

"What do *I* get if I make it?" Brian asked.

"I'll buy you a soda," Wendy said.

Brian nodded at her. Her smile alone might just be worth it. Like before, he slammed the board forward, leaning into the drop. Down one ramp, across the flat, and then shooting up the other side. He tapped the far side lip, spun around, and rolled back the other way.

"He can't do it!" Frankie shouted. "Look, he didn't get no air! He did it same as before."

Brian rolled up the ramp, whipping a quick kickturn, building speed. Fast now, up to the other side, and then back down across the flat. He was ready. He'd done it before. He'd go for air on the next pass.

Up the transition to the lip by the guys. Turn and —

Someone kicked the back end of his board and the wheels scraped sideways. *Spitfire* wobbled into the drop. Brian flailed his arms and tried to keep his balance, but he was off center and fell. A sharp pain shot up from his elbow as he hit the ramp hard and tumbled into the flat. The skateboard rolled up the far transition and then back down, smacking him in the back.

"Hee hee hee hee heeeeeeee! Wipeout!" Frankie sang the old song off pitch, making a sweeping motion with the toe of his boot.

"Frankie, you idiot!" Wendy shouted.

"Oh, come on. I was just joking around!"

Brian clenched his fists. It was the perfect run until this jerk messed it up. He stood up. "What's your problem?"

The other guys went quiet. Frankie stopped laughing. He slid on his feet down the ramp and shoved him hard in the chest. "*You're* my problem." He was breathing heavy and glaring at Brian. "And now I'm gonna be *your* problem." Frankie pushed him again.

Wendy moved up closer. "Stop it, Frankie!"

Frankie was so short and stood so close that he had to look up at Brian, but as he kept his big arms partly cocked back, Brian could tell he had been lifting weights. Worse, there was a little twitch in his eye that made him look like he could go off at any moment. This was not the kind of guy Brian wanted to throw down with, not right now. His foot found *Spitfire*.

"Time to teach you a lesson," Frankie said, balling up his fist. He lunged forward, but Brian was quick, jumping back as he pushed *Spitfire* under Frankie's foot. Frankie slipped on the skateboard and went reeling backward, slamming down onto the flat bottom and hitting his head.

As he lay there for a moment, Alex rushed up to Brian. He whispered, "You got guts, but seriously, you should go."

It would look bad to run from a fight, but there was no way this could end well. Brian ran to his board, jumped on, and kick-started off, cutting tight around the back of the half-pipe and shooting down the sidewalk the way he had come in. He'd only been in Riverside for a few days and had no idea where to go next. Worse, the town was built on one big hill. Getting to his house, to Grandpa's, or even just to the town square would be an uphill run.

Brian skated out onto the road, clearing the end of the block and shooting through the T intersection where Weigand Street met the highway. He glanced back, and Frankie was up and following on his own skateboard. Brian kicked at the street to go faster. How was he ever going to get out of this? Unless Frankie made a mistake and crashed somehow, there was really no way to escape. And if Frankie caught him . . .

He checked his six. Frankie was starting to close the gap. Brian pushed harder. Without thinking, he cut a tight corner, heading downhill toward the river. A grove of trees temporarily kept him out of Frankie's sight, but the tough guy would round the corner in no time.

"Brian!" A kid on a big blue two-seat bike shot out of the trees and pulled up alongside him, surprising him so much that he almost waxed out. With his black-rimmed glasses and dark hair, the bike rider looked like Harry Potter without the cool scar. "Grab on," the kid said.

Whoever he was, he was Brian's best chance to get away. Brian took hold of the back handlebars and sighed as he relaxed his legs for a moment.

The rider risked a look back, sunlight flashing bright off

his thick glasses. "I'm Max Warrender. I presume you are Brian Roberts?"

Brian nodded.

"I thought so," the kid said. "It's nice to meet you, Brian." He faced forward and kept pedaling furiously down the hill.

"Yeah, um, nice to meet you too," Brian said. He glanced behind him again. Frankie was still on the other side of the trees, but he'd be in sight any moment. And Max was providing all the power for both of them on this heavy bike.

"Um, Frankie's right behind us," Brian said. "We can't get away from him going straight down this road. He'll catch up to us eventually."

"He will find it extraordinarily difficult to do so."

"What?"

Max shot him a serious look. "You need to hold on to those handlebars very tightly."

"Um . . ." What did this guy think he was doing? "Okay?"

Max tilted his head to the side. "How fast can a skateboard travel before the ball bearings in the wheels strip out?" He shrugged. "Oh well." He reached down and flipped a switch on the tip of a big metal pole that he'd mounted on the other side of the bike.

A sound like a cannon exploded right next to Brian, and the bike shot forward so fast that he almost lost his grip on the handlebars. When he focused again, fire was erupting from the end of the tube. A rocket! How could there be a rocket? On a bike!

Max took his feet off the pedals and laughed as the bike roared down the highway. "Warp speed!"

They flew past a wooden sign with a picture of the starship *Enterprise* and the words *Where the Trek Begins,* across a bridge over the river and out into the country. Cornfields melted into blurs on either side of the road. Brian had to lean back while holding the handlebars just to keep the board under his body.

The wind blew through his hair as they passed fields, farms, and pastures. Frankie was nowhere in sight, and Riverside itself seemed to shrink in the distance. But the rocketbike still sped up, faster and faster and faster. When they zipped up over a hill, just for a moment, the bike and skateboard actually left the pavement. Brian loved the leap in his stomach as he soared through the air.

"Woo!" His heart was thumping as the bike and *Spitfire* touched down. "Max, I think we're safe now," he shouted as loud as he could to be heard over the roar of the wind and the rocket. "Can you slow down?" If his skateboard's wheels seized up, the board would grind to a halt, yanking him off the bike and tossing him to the pavement.

"It's a solid-fuel rocket, Brian," Max called back. "I'm afraid it will increase speed until it has exhausted its fuel supply!"

This is crazy, Brian thought. If he let go of the bike, could he keep the shaking skateboard under control long enough to slow down? Maybe, but maybe not. He'd have to ride it out.

At last the rocket began to fizzle. It sputtered and emitted two last bursts of flame before the fire cut out completely, with just a thick grayish-white smoke rolling out of the back.

"Can you slow it down now?" Brian shouted.

"I'll try." Max pulled the hand brakes. The brakes squeaked and smoked when they made contact with the rims of the wheels. "We have too much velocity. There's too much friction on the wheel." He kept pumping the brakes, though, applying pressure, letting go, and then braking again. The bike slowed down until they finally came to a full stop.

Brian unclamped his hands from the back handlebars, fingers aching. They were on a bridge over a small creek, and he staggered with shaky legs to sit on the big steel guardrail by the side of the road. Max walked his bike over to join him. Smoke still rolled out of the end of the rocket.

"Thanks, Max. You know, for helping me get away from —"

"Stand by!" Max dumped the bike on the ground with the rocket side up. The rocket was making a quiet hissing sound — a small whistle that seemed to be getting louder and higher pitched. Brian noticed the boxy black letters *NX-02* painted on the side of the rocket.

"Oh no! Not again. Just like the NX-01!" Max grabbed one of the clamps on the metal bands securing the rocket to the bike. He grunted as he yanked on it. "Try to get the other one loose."

"Why?"

Max pulled on the clamp again. "It's critical to remove this rocket quickly."

Brian grabbed the other one and tugged hard. It gave a little bit. In another pull he had the clamp released and the metal band off. Max had done the same. Now the whistle had reached a crescendo with a horrible, high-pitched shriek.

"Why is it making that noise?" Brian shouted.

Max grabbed one end of the rocket. "Pick that up! Hurry!" Brian lifted the other end. It was surprisingly light. They sidestepped to the edge of the bridge. "Throw it!"

They heaved the rocket over the side. Max dropped to the pavement and Brian followed. They heard a splash and then the *crack* of an enormous explosion blasting from below. Water and mud splattered down all over them.

Brian stood up, wiping some globs of mud off his shirt. He followed Max to look over the side of the bridge. Water was rushing in to fill a new crater in the bottom of the creek bed.

"What was that all about?" Brian asked.

Max frowned as he watched the water run into the hole. "I'm not sure," he said. "It's possible that I didn't pack the fuel mixture correctly. Or else the internal heat shield is overheating and sealing up the exhaust port, causing an overpressure. I can never tell, because all I ever have left to analyze are small fragments."

"You mean you made that thing? You've done this before?" Brian could hardly believe it. "And what's with the markings? NX-02?"

"It was a reference to the TV show *Star Trek: Enterprise*," Max said.

Brian nodded. It had sounded familiar. One of the best things about moving to Riverside was that it was famous for being the future birthplace of *Star Trek* Captain James T. Kirk.

"My mother is Dr. Mary Warrender, your father's partner in Synthtech," said Max. "Your mother sent me down from your house to bring you home for the investor presentation." He pointed toward the trees. "Come on. The abandoned railroad tracks run back in those woods. We can follow them in case Frankie's waiting for us on the road."

"Lead the way," Brian said.

Max walked his bike down into the ditch toward the trees, and Brian followed. A breeze rustled through the corn stalks. He could see Riverside's church steeple and grain elevator in the distance. It was all so different from Seattle. He ran his fingers back through his hair. "Thanks for helping me get away from Frankie," he said. He owed Max that, even if the escape had almost killed him.

"It was my pleasure," said Max. "It was also a good opportunity to try out my latest rocket. Clearly there's still some work to do," he mumbled.

They walked up the slope to the tracks and headed toward town. Tall trees and thick shrubs lined either side of the railroad bed. Neither one spoke for a while as they walked. The only sound was the bumping of Max's bike tires on the wooden ties.

Brian finally broke the quiet. "Why did you do all this anyway?"

"I find rockets rather fascinating. Ever since —"

"No, I mean, why did you help me get away from Frankie?"

"I have had some unpleasant encounters with Frankie in the past," Max said. "The more frustrated he becomes, the more dangerous he is, and he looked rather angry when your skating was superior."

Brian's goal in going to the skate park was to meet people and make friends. It hadn't gone the way he'd expected, but who could expect a rocketbike? He looked at Max and smiled. "Well, thanks for an awesome ride." He had made one friend, at least.

"Welcome to Riverside," Max said.

Thanks to the rocketbike adventure and the long walk home, Brian and Max were late. They entered through the back door into the kitchen as quietly as they could. Brian could hear his father and Max's mom giving their presentation in the living room.

His own mother was at the counter making drinks. "Brian, where were you? Your father was hoping to introduce you at the start of the presentation. Why are you all dirty? Never mind," she said before he could answer. "Just get upstairs and change. I put a shirt out for you."

Brian led the way to his room, where Max nodded toward the *Let It Be* poster as he took a seat at the desk. "Who are these guys?"

"Are you serious?" Brian said. "The Beatles." Max stared at him blankly. Brian shook his head. "From England? Huge in the sixties? John Lennon? Paul McCartney?"

"I mostly enjoy listening to the instrumental sound-tracks from the *Star Trek* films," said Max. "Also Weird Al Yankovic. His songs are very humorous."

Brian picked up the new shirt Mom had bought him for tonight. It was white with buttons and an annoying collar.

Max leaned forward and looked at Brian's model jet. "This is excellent work."

"Thanks," Brian said.

"The SR-71 Blackbird still holds the record for the fastest jet plane. It could exceed Mach Three. That's roughly two thousand three hundred miles per hour. At top speed, the Blackbird could cross Iowa in . . ." He poked his finger around in the air as if writing calculations on an invisible chalkboard. "Under ten minutes."

"Wow," Brian said. "That's a lot of information."

Max shrugged. "I could tell you more." He put the model down. "The details are painted with remarkable accuracy."

"My grandfather gave me that kit for Christmas last year." It had been one of just a few gifts he'd received, with Mom and Dad's money tied up in Synthtech.

"Are you interested in aircraft?" Max ran his finger along one of the big engines on the sleek black spy plane.

"Oh yeah!" Brian slipped the shirt on. "My dad's got his pilot's license, and we used to own a single-engine airplane. A Cessna Cardinal II." He smiled, remembering the pre-flight checks with Dad while the Beatles played on Dad's CD player. He thought of the fun of taking the Cardinal up flying some weekends. There was nothing like checking out Mount Saint Helens from the air.

"It seems as if you and your father are close."

"Yeah, I guess so, but we don't do as many fun things as we used to."

"Both of my parents have important jobs at the University of Iowa," Max said proudly. "My mother is a professor of chemical engineering. My father works in the senior levels of administration and finance." His enthusiasm faded, and he looked down, speaking more quietly. "They sometimes have time to assist me with especially difficult mathematical or scientific enquiries, but they prefer that I work things out on my own."

Brian buttoned his shirt. Max did "mathematical or scientific enquiries" at home? What must life be like for him?

"Do you miss flying?" Max asked after a brief quiet.

"Well, yeah," Brian said, grateful for the subject change. "It used to be tons of fun. Plus, we'd go to air shows all the time, see antique planes and stuff. We even toured an old World War Two B-17 bomber." He paused. "But Dad had to sell the Cardinal to help pay for the company." Brian threw his dirty shirt in the hamper. "He's always busy now."

Someone knocked on the door. It was probably time to go downstairs for Dad's whole impress-the-rich-lady meeting thing. "Come in," Brian said.

It was Grandpa. "Ah, Brian, I see Max found you without too much trouble. Hope you boys are getting along okay." Grandpa lived on a farm at the edge of town. He kept this house as a rental property and was letting Brian's parents live there for free since money was tight. "Anyway, good news, boys. I've talked to your folks. They said you only needed to be here for the initial introduction. But . . ." He coughed a little. "Since you missed that, we're just going to skip this whole thing. I'll take you both out for ice cream and then to my farm for a bit. You can have leftovers for dinner later tonight."

"Thank you, Mr. Davis," Max said quietly. He stood up and hurried out of the room.

Brian scrambled back out of his uncomfortable shirt and pulled on his *Yellow Submarine* T-shirt.

Grandpa cleared his throat. "Listen, Brian . . ."

Uh-oh. Whenever an adult started a conversation with "Listen, Brian," a big, serious lecture was bound to follow.

"I'll try to keep this short. I know that you probably just lost track of time, but your father had really been hoping you could be here for this meeting. He wanted to show you off to that lady down there, Mrs. Whatshername." He grinned. "Now, I'm not trying to make you feel bad about tonight. Just telling you that these next few months, your parents are going to be very busy, maybe a little tense, while your father is getting this business up and running. You're going to be on your own some, and I need you to promise to help out and be on your best behavior."

Brian nodded. It was a good thing he'd done that whole almost-get-in-a-fight thing *before* he had to make this promise.

Grandpa reached over to muss his hair. "Good man."

Downstairs, Grandpa stopped them in the dining room so they wouldn't interrupt the presentation. He spotted Mom in the kitchen and went to talk to her. Max looked impatient to leave, but as long as they had to wait for Grandpa, Brian peeked into the living room to watch Dad work his business magic.

Dad was dressed in his jeans and a suit-type coat, standing in front of a big screen. Dr. Warrender stood next to him in black dress pants, a shiny purple shirt, and a black jacket with shoulder pads. Her dark hair was pulled back tightly and she wore the same sort of glasses as Max. Another man, wearing a tan jacket with fancy brown patches on the elbows — probably Max's father, with hair just like his son's — sat stiffly at the end of the couch.

A short woman with shoulder-length gray-flecked black hair was seated on a chair facing the screen. She handed a plate of food to a little man next to her and stood up as if to speak.

"Do you need something, Mrs. Douglas?" Dad said.

"Yes, Mr. Roberts." Mrs. Douglas put her hands on her hips. "Proof." She paused for a moment, and the room was completely silent. Dad's smooth smile didn't fade at all.

"The idea is intriguing, and you're a charming man. But if charm made money, I'd be a billionaire by now, and I won't be razzle-dazzled by scientific figures, some charts, and a lot of vague promises. That didn't work with any of my three ex-husbands or hubby number four here" — she nodded toward the man sitting next to her — "and it certainly won't work with you."

Dad chuckled as if the woman had just told a joke. "Mrs. Douglas, I certainly didn't mean to —"

"You know why I agreed to come down for this meeting?"

"Well, you strike me as a sharp businesswoman who knows a great opportu —"

"Cut the donkey diddle, Mr. Roberts. I got so much money now, I have to hire accountants just to monitor my accountants. I do little side projects like this for fun."

This little "side project" was a company that Brian's parents were risking everything for. What must it be like to have money like Mrs. Douglas had? She was still talking.

"Now I come here and you show me a lot of boring facts and figures. You have no proof. No demonstration. I'm not having any fun with this. You gotta impress me."

Max's mother took a small step forward. "I assure you, Mrs. Douglas, that Plastisteel is a very impressive substance. With your money to help us develop faster and more efficient ways of manufacturing it —"

"I expected to see a car made out of this magic plastic of yours. You can't even make me a wagon!"

Dr. Warrender fidgeted with a sparkly pin on her lapel. "We did have samples to show you, but we had a bit of a security —"

Dad clapped his hands. "Security in knowing that Plastisteel is so great that we, um . . . don't need samples. It's fantastic enough without samples!"

Mom entered the living room. "Mrs. Douglas, dinner's about ready. If you'd like to come into the dining room, we could get started."

Dad gave Mom a grateful look. "Ah, let's all head into the dining room, and we'd be happy to answer any more of your questions over dinner."

Grandpa pushed Brian and Max out the door before Mrs. Douglas could see them. When they had all climbed into his truck and he'd started the engine, he leaned back in his seat. "Whew!" He pulled a cigar from his pocket and held it in his teeth, then flicked his lighter open and puffed the cigar to life. "I thought we'd never get out of there. That investor woman was almost tougher than some of my old army drill sergeants."

Brian relaxed and enjoyed the warm smell from Grandpa's cigar. "Don't worry, my dad can handle anything."

Max only looked back toward the house.

Grandpa rolled his window down to let the smoke out,

put the truck into gear, and started to drive. They soon reached his house on the west edge of town. Instead of turning into his driveway, though, he pulled the truck over and parked on the street. Grandpa blew out a long puff, flicked his ashes out the window, and then set the cigar in the truck's ashtray. "We have arrived."

"What are we doing?" Brian asked. "I thought we were going to get ice cream."

"Want to introduce you to my neighbor boy here across the street. He's a good guy. Does chores for me around the farm sometimes." Grandpa put his hand to his back and groaned as he climbed down out of the truck.

Brian wasn't totally thrilled by the idea of his grandpa introducing him around, but Grandpa was already halfway up the path to the front door. He waited for Max to open the passenger door so he could get out.

"I do not believe this is the wisest course of action," Max said.

"Can't stop him now, though," Brian said. He scooted across the seat to climb out the driver's side door, then hurried to catch up with Grandpa. Max followed slowly behind.

A moment after Grandpa rang the doorbell, the door opened, and Brian realized why Max had thought this was a bad idea. Out stepped Alex, the gambler from the skate park.

"Hey, Mr. Davis," said Alex. He leaned to see around Grandpa and spotted Brian and Max. "Um . . . hey," he said to Brian. He nodded. "Max."

"Hello, Alex! I think you know Max Warrender here, but I want you to meet my grandson Brian," Grandpa said. Brian tried to smile, though he felt a little strange being introduced to someone he already knew. Max just stared at the ground. Grandpa patted Brian on the back. "He just moved to town and will be starting sixth grade with you and Max tomorrow. I figured you'd all have a lot in common and maybe you'd like to come get ice cream with us. My treat. Then you might show Brian and Max around the farm, since you've gotten so familiar with it, working there this summer."

"Sounds great," Alex said.

Soon all four of them squeezed into Grandpa's truck and headed out toward the Tasty Freeze drive-in. Grandpa said he was fine with his cigar, but he bought a chocolate ice-cream cone for Alex, vanilla for Max, and a chocolate-and-vanilla twist for Brian.

"Thanks for this," Alex said when they were in the truck on the way back.

"Yeah, this is great, Grandpa," said Brian. Grandpa nodded.

Max didn't say anything, and a quiet settled over the cab.

"Brian here is pretty good on the skateboard," Alex said.

"Is that right?"

Brian felt his cheeks go hot. If Alex told Grandpa about the near fight with Frankie, Grandpa would worry again about him staying out of trouble.

"Best skateboarder I've ever seen," Alex said. Brian smiled.

"I've seen some of those boys at the skate park." Grandpa flicked ash out the window. "I don't understand how they can go so fast on those things."

Max grinned behind his ice-cream cone, and Brian nodded at him. Grandpa had no idea just how fast a skateboard could go.

Finally, Grandpa pulled the truck into the gravel driveway back at his farm. He reached over and crushed his cigar out in the ashtray. "You boys have fun and take a look around. I've got to check on some things in the house."

Then it was just the three of them, standing out in the driveway, licking their ice-cream cones with the sun low in the west. Nobody said anything at first, and Brian made sure Grandpa had gone inside. "Thanks," he said to Alex.

Alex frowned over the top of his ice-cream cone. "For what?"

"For not telling my grandpa about Frankie, and for not being mad about me taking your money at the skate park."

"Your grandfather's totally cool," said Alex. "He pays really well for the garden work, mowing, and other jobs I do around here. And as for the money you won . . ." He laughed.

"If Frankie hadn't ruined all the action, I would have prob-ably made my ten bucks back on the commission."

"Your commission?" Brian asked.

Alex glanced at the door to the house, like he too wanted to make sure Grandpa was really gone. "I arrange and keep track of all the bets in our class. Then I take a five percent cut of all the winnings." He started toward the barn, motion-ing for Brian and Max to follow. "Five percent may not sound like much, but it adds up. Basically —" He took a huge bite out of his crunchy cone and spoke with his mouth full. "I never lose."

Brian followed Alex into the barn. A couple horses shifted in a stall in the back. The stinging, salty smell of manure burned his nose and eyes as Alex led him to a wooden ladder in the middle of the building.

Brian stopped when he noticed Max had fallen so far behind. "Max, you coming?" he called.

Alex started up the ladder. "Yeah, Mad Max, hurry up."

Max sighed and joined them. Brian watched them both. Something in Alex's voice and Max's slowness and silence was sounding alarm bells in his mind.

"Come on," Alex called down from up in the hayloft. "You'll love this."

Brian and Max joined him. Giant bales of hay were neatly piled to form a mountain all the way up to a big open-ing in the front wall near the roof. Bits of dust swirled in the beam of light. Max sneezed. Alex took hold of the end of a rope that hung from the rafters and climbed up near the top of the haystack. Brian backed off to the side to get out of the way.

Gripping the rope in both hands, Alex took a running leap off the hay, swinging a dozen feet above the floor of the loft. He kicked his legs at the farthest reach of his swing, then swooped back to land on the haystack. "Dude! You have to try this."

It did look fun. Brian climbed the hay, took the rope, and stared at the big empty space down in front of him.

"Scared?" Alex asked Brian.

"Nope," Brian answered. This seemed just like pulling off a skating trick. If he took too long, he'd end up skater spooked. He ran back a few paces, then sprinted forward and pushed off as hard as he could. Out into the air, swooping like he was falling, down toward the wood floor, then up and away toward the other side of the barn. The horses whinnied in their stalls far below, but he flew over them, untouchable. At the far end of the swing he seemed to hang there, weightless and floating, before gliding back through the air to land on the hay. "Awesome!"

"Good swing," Alex said.

"Want to try it, Max?" Brian said.

Max shook his head. He was standing off to the side with his arms folded over his chest. He looked angry or sad or something.

Brian frowned. "Come on, Max, it's like flying. Or as close to flying as I've been since my dad sold his plane." He looked up to the dusty rafters. "I just wish the barn roof was a lot higher. We could get an even bigger swing."

"I appreciate the offer," said Max. "However, I'm okay just watching."

Alex rolled his eyes. "Whatever, Mad Max."

Max let out a long breath. He took off his glasses and rubbed his eyes. "Do you miss flying, Brian?"

Was he serious? Brian launched another swing, kicking his legs at the far end before sailing back to the hay bales. "I miss it more than anything. There's nothing better than —"

"If you want to fly, let me show you something." Max went down the ladder before Brian or Alex could ask another question.

Brian shrugged and started to go after him. He stopped halfway down the ladder when he noticed Alex hadn't moved. "You coming?"

Alex shrugged too and made for the ladder. "I guess so."

Max waited for them at the bottom.

"Where are we going?" Alex said.

Max led them out of the barn, then down to a large shed by the barbed-wire fence on the west edge of the property. He peeked around the far corner to the house, checking to make sure Brian's grandpa wasn't watching, then turned back. "I want to show you what I have inside this building."

Alex let out a loud sigh. "Nobody has been in this old shed for years, Max. The padlock on the doors is all rusted. We'd have to cut the lock to get in."

"I never said I entered through the door."

"Oh, what? Did one of your dorky *Star Trek* books show you how to build a transporter?"

That was mean, but Max didn't seem to notice. He pushed back a branch from a raspberry bush and lifted a piece of plywood to reveal a big hole dug out beside the wall. "We enter through here."

Alex bent down to look closer. "What is that? Some kind of animal den?"

"No," said Max. "I just go in through —"

"Oh, Mad Max," Alex said, "you're lucky that whatever dug that didn't claw your face off." He chuckled. "It could have been a badger, Max. A badger would have killed you."

"It's not a badger den," Max said.

"It could be," Alex said.

"Badgers aren't even indigenous to this area. They mostly live in —"

"Who cares about badgers?" Brian said. "Who cares what dug the stupid thing? What's inside?"

Max looked hurt. "Well, I dug it. It's a tunnel. Follow me." He crawled down into the hole. The last thing Brian could see were Max's legs sticking out from under the wall, almost like the first dead witch in *The Wizard of Oz*.

"This is stupid. I'm going home," said Alex.

"Don't you want to see whatever it is he's so excited about?"

Alex shook his head. "Listen, man. You're new here. The rest of us have lived here forever. Max used to be okay when we were little kids, like playing with toys and building forts and stuff." He picked up a small rock and threw it across the fence into the field. "But then he got all nerdy. He's too smart for his own good. Nobody cool really hangs around him. He actually put on a *Star Trek* uniform and shaved his head to be Captain Kirk at Trekfest last June."

Captain Kirk was never bald. "You mean Captain Picard?"

Alex raised an eyebrow. "Dude. Seriously."

Brian turned away toward the tunnel. Stupid. Alex was clearly a cool guy, the sort of friend Brian needed if he wanted to make more friends in this place. Hopefully he'd forget what Brian had just said. He also hoped Max hadn't heard any of it. He couldn't just leave Max in there waiting. But if he went in alone, Alex might think Brian was just like Max.

"I'll give your five bucks back if you go in there with me," Brian said.

"What?" Alex asked. "Why?"

"I just . . . I don't want to go in by myself."

"Good point." Alex motioned toward the hole. "You first."

Brian took a deep breath and crawled down into the tunnel.

The tunnel was about two feet deep and nearly three feet wide. Brian ran his hands along the smooth walls and floor. The dirt had been hardened with some kind of clear sealant, so there was no dust or loose pebbles. The floor of the shack was cut out next to the wall, so he entered the building as soon as he stood up.

"Oh . . . wow."

He had expected to find a dusty tool shed full of shovels and rakes, maybe an old lawn mower. Instead, he had emerged into what looked like a science lab. A white sheet hung over something on a wood table in the center of the room. Whatever was under the sheet was so big that it stuck out past the edge of the table on both sides. Technical diagrams, blueprints, and complex mathematical equations with some symbols Brian had never even seen covered the walls. There wasn't a speck of dust or a cobweb anywhere.

On a big wood workbench on the far wall was another rocket like the one from Max's bike. A life-size Captain Kirk cardboard cutout stood next to the bench. Model airplanes and a few model starships hung from the ceiling. Brian recognized some little biplanes, the starship *Enterprise*, a couple jets, a Romulan warbird — even the SR-71 Blackbird.

"What is all this?" Alex said as soon as he entered.

"Gentlemen," Max said. "Welcome to what I like to call the Eagle's Nest."

"The Eagle's Nest?" Alex asked.

Max shrugged. "It sounds better than 'secret workshop.'"

Whatever Max called it, it was well equipped. Another workbench ran the length of the wall under which Max had tunneled. That held a huge assortment of tools: saws, screwdrivers, hammers, sanders, chisels, pliers, clamps, soldering irons, even a big vise on the end.

"Is this a computer?" Alex was looking over a bunch of hardware on a table at the south end of the shed. A couple of screens, a keyboard, and three computer towers had been opened up and wired together. "Did you build this thing yourself?"

Max nodded. "It's a hybrid, constructed from several older models that my father was no longer using. The three computers working together form an impressively efficient system."

"You got Internet?" Alex asked. Max nodded again. Alex examined the computer more closely. "Yeah, but how? You couldn't call the Internet company and have them install it in a secret workshop."

"I'm picking up wireless."

"From who?" Brian asked. "My grandpa isn't online."

Max took off his glasses and chewed the end of the earpiece. "That's not important."

"My house," Alex said. "You're stealing Internet from the wireless at my house across the street."

Max put his glasses back on. "It's not really stealing when people don't password protect their wireless routers."

Alex folded his arms over his chest. "It'll be password locked from now on, Mad Max. Believe me."

"Max, how did you get all this stuff in here?" Brian asked. "It wouldn't fit through the tunnel."

Max went to the north end and tapped a small metal plate on one of the big double doors. "The padlock on the outside is rusted nearly solid, but if I take out a few screws, the whole locking mechanism falls off outside. I brought the big stuff in through the doors when it was dark or when Brian's grandpa was away."

"And you've been using his electricity," Brian said. "How long have you been breaking in here like this?"

Max fidgeted. "I realize this could be construed as criminal trespassing, but it was the only place I could find in town to work on all of this in secret."

Brian looked at the diagrams, the model airplanes, and the sheet-covered thing on the table in the center of the room. It all pointed toward the impossible . . . except that Max had already proved he was pretty smart and resourceful, the kind of guy who could build a mostly successful rocketbike. He grabbed the sheet and yanked it away.

"Oh wow," Brian whispered again.

A real airplane rested on the table. This was no toy, no model. It was a full-size flyer, a low-winged aircraft like many he'd seen at the air shows he and his father used to attend — functional and well-assembled, unmistakably homemade, but with a certain elegance. She was constructed from gleaming white plastic, about eight feet from propeller to tail and nine feet from wingtip to wingtip. She reminded Brian of a soaring hawk, its head the engine up front, wings spread wide in the middle, and a light smaller tail rising up behind.

Almost afraid to touch her, he reached out slowly and spun the two-bladed propeller. "Is this a lawn mower engine?" The spark plug and pull start cable were in the right place, but it had been tipped on its left side, with its deck removed and a big plastic fuel tank to its right. The whole thing had been upgraded with a complex set of plastic tubes, cogs, and gears.

Max put his hand to the propeller to stop the spin. "It was a lawn mower, but I've created and installed smaller, lighter, stronger engine components that require less lubrication. The engine as originally designed had only one cylinder providing all its power. I've been able to add three more cylinders and improved engine efficiency enough that the flyer is up to about thirty horsepower, able to reach takeoff speed."

"Takeoff speed?" Alex said. "You don't think this thing will actually fly, do you? I mean, it has skateboards for wheels."

Brian smiled. Alex was right. Instead of regular wheels, this aircraft rested on two parallel skateboards situated about a foot apart. A support strut extended down from the engine to a bar bolted across the noses of the skateboards. Two other struts rose from the middle of the boards, attaching under the wings near the center of the aircraft.

"The tilt of the nose on each skateboard, as well as the curve of the engine cover and wings, provides the lift," Max said. "Also, despite their small size and light weight, skateboard wheels can handle the significant speed required for takeoff and landing."

"That's true." Brian remembered his rocket-towed ride on *Spitfire*. He ducked under the wing, admiring the perfect aerodynamic curve of its underside, then moved the aileron flap up and down.

"But there's no cockpit. No cabin," Alex said.

"There's not supposed to be a cabin on this aircraft," said Max. "It's completely open air."

Alex tapped one of the models. "You mean like this biplane, with the pilot's head sticking out the top?"

"No." Max reached up and put a hand on each of the two green plastic school desk chairs bolted to the central beam. "The pilot and copilot just sit in these chairs with their legs on either side."

"They ride it almost like a motorcycle?" Alex asked.

Max shrugged. "A flying motorcycle, I guess." A clear plastic windshield mounted on top of the engine casing protected the pilot, who would control the plane with the simple throttle, yoke, and foot pedals arranged in front of the seat.

Max went to a drawer in the desk under his computer and pulled out a toy *Star Trek* phaser. He pressed a button on the phaser, shooting a small red dot of light onto the white wings. He'd put a laser pointer into a *Star Trek* weapon. Alex elbowed Brian and rolled his eyes as Max continued. "The wings are at the balance point, the center of gravity on the aircraft." He shot the phaser at the engine. "The motor, though quite light, is still the heaviest component on the plane, so it's right in front of the wings, while the tail rudder assembly provides a counterbalance in the rear. It is a very small, simple, lightweight aircraft. It could be used by the military or even to replace the automobile."

"No kid would be able to build a real plane that works," said Alex.

"Like I always say, any problem can be overcome through proper research," said Max.

"Seriously?" Alex said. "You really always say that?"

Max's cheeks reddened a little, but he acted like he hadn't heard. "I just had to consider the ratio of the area and curvature of the wing to the lift force. I had to study engines and theorize how much horsepower would be required for flight in an aircraft of this nature. Information about all of this, data, plans, and schematics for various existing similar aircraft, can be found online and in books. It's simply a matter of the correct application."

"But the controls," said Alex. "My family and I flew to Mexico once, and I caught a look inside the cockpit. There were about a billion buttons and levers and things."

"That's for a big commercial jet," said Brian. "A little single-engine plane is much simpler. I used to go to air shows with my dad, and there were plenty of planes that weren't much more complicated than this." He shrugged.

"But I bet you never saw a plastic airplane at any of those shows," Alex said. "This thing is just a toy!"

"The majority of the flyer is actually constructed of Plastisteel." Max's eyes met Brian's for a moment, and then he looked away.

"Plastisteel?" Brian asked. "Like the Plastisteel your mom is working on?"

"You mean plastic?" said Alex.

Max folded his hands over his chest. "Plastisteel. It's the fusion of elements of steel into a dense polymer."

"English, please?" Alex said.

"Essentially, Plastisteel is an extraordinarily durable but very lightweight plastic."

"Dude, I think you need therapy," Alex said. "This is a cool model or whatever, and you might be smart, but there's no way plastic could be strong enough —"

Max held up his hands. "I assure you that you haven't seen anything like this before." He went to the end of the tool bench and cranked open the vise, then slipped a small piece of sheet metal in and clamped the vise tight. From under the bench he pulled out a big sledgehammer. "Here." He held the hammer out to Alex. "Please strike this piece of heavy aluminum as hard as you can."

Alex took the hammer. "This is stupid."

"Please just indulge me in this one thing. I promise you will be impressed."

Alex sighed. "Fine." He lifted the hammer and twisted back like a major league baseball player. Sparks fell as the sledge slammed into the sheet metal with a dull clang. Alex put the hammer down and Max released the vise. He held up the piece of metal, bent at a right angle where Alex had smashed it.

"Now let's try that again," said Max. He cranked the vise tight on a piece of white plastic. "This time with

Plastisteel. You will note that this sheet of Plastisteel is slightly thinner than the aluminum."

"Okay." Alex picked up the hammer and started to swing it again. "I don't see what the point of — OW!" The sledge crashed into the plastic and bounced back. He dropped the hammer.

Max took the white plastic out of the vise and held it and the metal up. "As you can see, this sheet of aluminum, similar to that used on most small aircraft, is completely bent as a result of the hammer impact. The Plastisteel, though lighter, thinner, and struck with approximately the same force, suffered much less damage, and is bent approximately an inch."

Alex rubbed his arms. "You could have warned me, Max! I feel like I just punched a solid wall."

"I apologize for the discomfort," Max said.

Brian held out his hand and Max gave him the piece of Plastisteel. So this was the stuff Dad had invested everything in. They'd left Seattle and come out to this tiny town in the corn for this special plastic. He extended it back to Max, but held on when Max tried to take it. "Where did you get this?"

Before Max could answer, Alex reached between them to spin the propeller. "Plastisteel construction. A rebuilt motor. You know, guys, if this could actually work . . ." He faced Max, rubbing his knuckles against his chin. "I'm seeing green here. Green as in money. People would go nuts to know that sixth grade boys built a plane and flew around in it."

Brian frowned. So now Alex suddenly thought this was cool?

"The construction is complete," Max said quickly. "What I really need are two people to serve as pilot and copilot."

"You mean, two people besides you?" Brian said.

"Um . . . precisely." Max's face was getting red. "I require a pilot and copilot. Two people besides me. I won't actually be flying it. You see, I'm acrophobic."

Alex frowned. "You're afraid of acrobats?"

"He's afraid of heights." Brian sat down on a stool by the table.

"You're afraid of heights, so you built your own airplane?" Alex asked.

"Last year at the science fair I did a project with a wind tunnel and various configurations of model planes. I worked hard on it." Max shrugged. "My parents said I did a thorough job, but it was a fairly unoriginal project. I wanted to take my research to the next level."

Brian thought this was the next level, all right. Could it really take off? The wings were raised as high as other low-winged aircraft he'd seen. Their size looked comparable to planes he'd seen too. It would be incredible to be at the controls, to not just sit in a plane with his father, but to pilot his own aircraft. To actually fly. Out in the open. Riding the sky. Brian ran his hands along one of the smooth wings. He looked up and saw Alex's and Max's big grins.

"Remember how awesome it was swinging on the rope?" Alex aimed little finger guns at Brian with both hands. "Now think of that, but on, like, the most vicious energy drink of your life!" He pushed his thumbs down, firing the guns. "Way higher. Me and you, flying in our own plane. A sophisticated, one-of-a-kind aircraft."

Brian grinned back. It was a long shot, but like Dad always said, "Great success comes only through great risk." "Let's do it," he said.

"All right!" Alex said. He fist-bumped with Brian, but Max only reached out as if to shake hands. Alex slapped him five instead. Brian laughed and then shook Max's hand. "So when do we fly?"

"The flyer is ready to fly now. We could conduct our first test flight tomorrow night after dark."

"A night flight?" Brian asked.

Max frowned. "I realize that flying at night doesn't offer the most ideal conditions. However, we'll need to take the flyer out of the Eagle's Nest through the double doors. We'll want to move after dark to avoid detection. In any case, the runway I have in mind is well lit and should facilitate a safe landing."

"Sweet," Alex said. "We're set to fly tomorrow night, then. Just tell your parents that you're going to my house to study or something. We'll meet here and wait for the sun to go down."

"Hey," Brian said. Thinking of his parents reminded him of the meeting they'd escaped earlier. "Didn't that rich lady say she would invest her money in Synthtech only if she was impressed or having fun or whatever?"

"I have no idea what you're talking about," Alex said.

Brian explained Synthtech's money troubles. "And she talked about a Plastisteel car, but what could be cooler than a Plastisteel plane? If we can fly this, as soon as Mrs. Douglas sees how awesome it is, she'll invest all kinds of money in Synthtech."

"As Mr. Spock might say, that's a logical approach," said Max.

"So dorky," Alex whispered. He shook his head. "Okay, but until the lady forks over the cash, we better keep this project quiet. If we lose control before we can publicize our flight, we won't make any money."

"Absolutely," Max said. "Secrecy is paramount. My parents have often warned me about the problems associated with discussing results before adequate experiments have been conducted."

Brian held his hand up. "So, until we've had our first successful test run, we work on this in secret. Nobody, not our parents, and especially not my grandfather, can ever find out about our workshop here."

"Awesome! Boys . . ." Alex rubbed his knuckles against his chin. "We'll make so much money. This is seriously great. We are going to fly."

After they crawled out of the Eagle's Nest, Alex and Max headed home. Grandpa drove Brian around town, going past the school and some other places to help him get acquainted with Riverside. Brian tried to be polite and interested in whatever Grandpa was telling him, but all he could think about was the chance to be up in the sky again.

When he finally walked into the living room at home, he was relieved to find the meeting was over. He sat down on the couch, still thinking about the flyer.

"Brian?" Dad spoke loudly.

"What?" Brian hadn't even noticed his father standing in the doorway of his office off the living room.

"I asked if you had a good time tonight. Didn't you hear me?"

"Sorry, Dad." Brian stood and followed his father into the office. "I guess I was distracted. Yeah, it was fun tonight. You were right about this being a chance to make new friends. I think I've already made two."

"Thattaboy!" Dad tipped back a glass of something bubbly and yellow, drinking it all down. "That's what I like to hear."

"How'd the meeting with the rich lady go?"

Dad shrugged. "Not as well as I had hoped."

"She's not going to invest?"

"She hasn't said yes *yet*," Dad said. "Just because someone says no one time doesn't mean the answer will *always* be no." He sat on the end of his desk. "Mrs. Douglas wants some flashy demonstration, but right now it will take us two months to make more Plastisteel. We're working on faster ways to manufacture it, but . . . Well, don't worry about it." He smiled. "I'll work it all out. No problem."

"I know you will." But Brian frowned. If Plastisteel took so long to make, how did Max get enough of it to make a plane? Maybe his Plastisteel was an early batch, some sort of prototype that wasn't up to Dad and Dr. Warrender's standards? It wouldn't matter after tomorrow night. Brian wished he could tell his father about how the flyer would prove Plastisteel's awesomeness to Mrs. Douglas, but he'd just made a promise of secrecy to the guys.

"I'm just glad to know you're off to a good start here in Riverside." Dad stood up off the desk and hugged him, patting him on the back. "You better get some sleep. Big day tomorrow."

A few minutes later, up in his bedroom, Brian tried to focus on his *Star Trek* book, but he kept remembering the way Alex had made fun of the show. He couldn't concentrate on a story set hundreds of years in the future when he was mainly concerned about tomorrow, his first day at a new school.

So far, things were going pretty great here. Max was a little nerdy, but crazy smart. Alex had seemed like he'd never get along with Max at first, but he was coming around. Two friends. The three of them almost made a decent group. He was still nervous — so nervous his stomach felt wrung out — but Brian figured his dad had the right attitude. He kept a positive outlook and kept trying even when he was challenged. That would be Brian's model for tomorrow. He hoped it would work.

Brian had given skateboarding a lot of thought over the years. It was not like riding in a car or on a bicycle. A bike was out in the open like a board, but you didn't feel the ride enough. On *Spitfire*, Brian felt like there was no vehicle carrying him at all, as if he simply glided down the streets and sidewalk on his own two feet. If he had to stop for traffic, he'd whip a tight kickturn with only his back wheels on the ground while the front end of his board spun around. Then he'd kick the board straight up in an ollie, jumping with the deck still pressed to his feet. If he could, he went for a slide, letting the bottom of his deck ride the edge of every bench. That's how he usually rolled, never passing up the chance for a trick. If he wanted a normal ride, he would ask his mom to drive him. Instead he skated it out. He wanted to fly.

This morning, however, he might as well have asked for a ride. As he rolled toward his first day at Riverside

Elementary, his stomach still felt hollow and twisted with nerves. Even the Beatles playing on his iPod couldn't get him going. He took an easy, wide, slow curve around the corner onto Lincoln Street.

A block and a half ahead, he saw the tough guy from the skate park, Frankie, walking with Wendy, the angel girl. She was wearing jeans and a gray shirt with some kind of white net shawl thing over it. Brian didn't feel like risking another round with Frankie this morning. He jumped off his board so they wouldn't hear him, then plucked out his earbuds and shut off his music.

Frankie put his arm around Wendy's shoulders and leaned over to say something close to her ear. "Frankie!" She laughed and pushed him away.

Brian watched in horror. How could an amazing girl like Wendy possibly be dating a guy like Frankie?

Frankie reached over and tickled her. She gasped in laughter and spun away from him. When she did, she spotted Brian, smiled, and waved. Brian weakly waved back. Frankie turned to see what Wendy was looking at. When he saw Brian, he stopped and stood straight up, his arms cocking back a little. Wendy started in Brian's direction, but Frankie grabbed her wrist and pulled her back. She twisted out of his grip, and the two of them argued quietly for a moment.

"Fine," Frankie said loudly. "See if I care." He stormed off ahead toward school.

Wendy shrugged and sort of skipped back to Brian. "Hey, it's the awesome skater! Ready for the first day? Are you nervous?"

"No, I'm cool," Brian lied. He had been a little nervous about starting a new school, and then Wendy had ditched her psychopath boyfriend to come talk to him. Now he was close to freaking out. He wiped his forehead and swallowed. "No big deal." This was already the longest outside-of-school conversation he'd ever had with a girl anywhere near this beautiful. The skateboard stunt must have done the trick.

They started walking again. "Sorry about yesterday with Frankie," Wendy said. "And for today too. He doesn't like me talking to guys."

"Yeah," he said. What was he supposed to say? "Some boyfriends are like —"

"Wait a minute," she said. "What did you say?"

"Nothing. Um . . . just that Frankie seems like one of those types of boyfriends who —"

"Gross!" Wendy shouted. She took two steps back from him and acted like she was going to throw up in the middle of the street. "I can *not* believe you!"

"What?" Brian worried for a moment that stuff was hanging out of his nose or something. "What did I say? Nothing. I'm sorry."

"Frankie is not, not, not, *not* my boyfriend!" She laughed. "He's my *brother*! I don't have a boyfriend."

"Oh." For a moment Brian was thrilled. Then he realized what a huge mistake he'd made, and he wished Max had built a time machine so that he could go back in time and avoid saying something so stupid.

She chuckled. "No, it's fine. He did put his arm around me, I guess. Ugh." Wendy stood straight. "Nice to meet you. I'm Wendy Heller."

"Brian Roberts."

She started again toward school. "Well, Brian Roberts, let's hope that's the most embarrassing thing that happens to you all day. Now tell me all about where you're from and how you learned to be such an awesome skater."

"I'm from Seattle," Brian said. "My family moved here for my dad's business. And skateboarding . . . Um, I don't know. I've been doing it a long time. I fell down a lot."

He would have kicked himself if he could. Why did he always say such dumb stuff, especially around girls? He risked a sideways glance at Wendy, but she wasn't laughing at him.

"Do you miss Seattle? How do you like Iowa so far?"

"Riverside seems like a pretty good place." He thought of the flyer. "I think I might really like it here."

Wendy shrugged. "It's okay, I guess. It used to be a lot better."

"What do you mean?"

"Nothing." She shook her head and looked happy again. "Who do you have for a teacher? Gilbert or Brown?"

"Um, Gilbert," Brian said. That's the name Mom said she got at registration.

"Cool! Me too." They were in front of the school now. Buses and cars pulled into the parking lot to unload. Wendy leaned closer to him and spoke in a low tone that sent tingles up Brian's neck. "Be careful, though. Gilbert's a little strict." She held the front door open and motioned Brian through. "After you."

Just as he went inside, a voice behind them shrieked, "Oh my gosh, Wendy, how *are* you?" A skinny girl with really long blond hair suddenly had her arms around Wendy's neck and half rode her into the building. "I haven't seen you in *so* long!"

"Hi, Abbie." Wendy laughed a little and gently unlocked Abbie's grip.

A different girl rounded the corner from another hallway and ran up to the two girls. She drew both of them to her in a big hug. "Wendy! Abbie!"

"Heather," Wendy said, less enthusiastically.

"Hey, Heather!" said Abbie.

"Oh my gosh, Wendy, that poncho is so cute! You guys, I've hardly seen you all summer." Abbie took them both by the hand. "I have *so* much to tell you. Come on!" She pulled Wendy and Heather away. Wendy looked back at Brian and shrugged.

Why did girls always make such a big deal out of seeing each other again? Brian wondered. It didn't matter if they had been apart all summer or for just a week. Whenever they were reunited, there were always hugs and high-pitched screeching and giggling. Brian's old dog used to freak out almost the same way every time Brian came home from school. That was the way of the wolf pack.

A sign hanging from the ceiling said the cafeteria, gym, fourth, fifth, and sixth grades were located in the wing to his right. Brian headed down the hall toward the sixth grade classrooms, but suddenly, he felt a hard pull on his backpack and was yanked sideways through a door. Before he knew what was happening, he was spun around so fast that he dropped *Spitfire*.

Frankie was in his face, grabbing the front of his shirt. Brian tried to shove him off, but the other boy just pushed him back against a steel railing. Behind him was a six-foot drop down to a cement floor and a huge steel boiler. Frankie shoved him so far over the railing that Brian had to grab Frankie's arms to keep from falling. Brian kicked him, and Frankie groaned, letting go with one hand. Brian's left arm flailed as he started to go over the railing.

Frankie pulled him back and shook him. "I got your attention?"

Brian hated feeling so helpless. "Let me go," he said.

"Oh yeah?" Frankie chuckled. "No problem." He jerked his arms like he was dropping him. Brian gasped, and Frankie gritted his teeth. "You listening now?"

Brian nodded.

"Good." Frankie pulled him up a little so he could look Brian in the eye. "I'm glad I don't have to bruise you up today. Then I'd have to listen to a fit from Wendy. But I *will* bruise you if I have to." His eye twitched. "Basically, it's real simple. I don't like show-offs who think they're so great on my skate ramp. I don't like punk new kids who don't know their place. Most of all, I hate weirdo freaks who talk to Wendy. So this is your one free pass. Stay away from my sister, and stay out of my way." Frankie pulled hard and brought him back upright on the top landing of the staircase. "Or else next time . . ."

He shoved Brian back against the steel railing and left him in the boiler room, the metal door clanging shut behind him.

Brian took deep breaths, trying to make his legs stop shaking and his stomach settle down. His grip on the rail tightened until his knuckles were white. A part of him wanted to run after Frankie and punch him right now. But he'd never been in a fight in his life, and he'd promised Grandpa he'd stay out of trouble. Plus, what Frankie lacked in size, he made up for in strength and quickness.

If only Brian could skip class and stay here in the boiler room. Or hide out in the bathroom. Or just go back home to Seattle.

Brian rested his head over his folded arms on the railing. Those were crazy ideas. His father would be ashamed of him for even thinking them. Dad always charged ahead, taking the big risks to chase after something great. Brian just needed to make himself go to class.

When he did finally get to Mrs. Gilbert's classroom, he was glad to see some familiar people. Alex nodded to him when he came in. Two desks behind Alex, Max looked up from a thick book. The light shone on his glasses, and he grinned broadly. From the other side of the room near the windows, Wendy offered a little wave, and Brian felt something inside him somersault. He smiled and nodded, grateful that Frankie was not around.

"I don't know, David," Alex said to a guy in the next row. "Riverside might have a good football team this year, but I think it's a little early to start talking about state championships."

David slapped his hand on his desk. "I'm telling you, they're going to be awesome. They have six returning varsity seniors and four juniors. They didn't have to bring up many sophomores."

"Just because your brother is quarterback . . ." said a red-haired kid who'd been at the skate park. He leaned over his desk with his knees on his chair.

David frowned. "Shut up, Red. Even if Matt wasn't quarterback, they'd still dominate."

Max cleared his throat. "Statistically speaking, when taking into account last year's football success and analyzing the performance of —"

"Analyze this!" Red threw a ball of crumpled paper, hitting Max right between the eyes. The guys all laughed.

"So dorky, Max," said David.

Brian slowly made his way toward the guys, but he didn't know where he was supposed to sit. He stood there, holding his backpack and skateboard, hoping nobody was paying any attention.

"David may be right," said a guy whose large size filled up all the space at his desk. "The football team had a start-of-season supper at Piggly's. My dad sold more barbecue pork that night than he did even on the Fourth of July. I thought the team looked pretty tough." He must have noticed Brian watching him. He flashed a big grin, his chins bunching up. "Hey, I'm Aaron Pineeda. Most people call me B.A. for short."

Brian frowned. "B.A.?"

"For 'Big Aaron.'"

Alex pulled his iPhone from a pocket inside his binder. "I don't know, guys." He pointed at something on the screen. "We have to play Dysart for the home opener Friday night. The Dysart Trojans went undefeated last year."

David threw his hands up. "They only beat us by two touchdowns. We're even better now. We can take 'em."

"Well, five dollars says we lose the opener."

"You'd bet against our own team?" Red asked.

"Just business." Alex leaned toward David. "So how about it?"

"I don't know," David said. "I don't have that much money."

"But you were so sure we'll win the state championship." Alex shrugged. "If you don't even think they'll win the first game . . ."

David sighed. "Fine. I bet you five bucks that the Roughriders win Friday night."

Alex and David shook hands and Alex keyed in the wager on his phone.

"Alex, are you always scheming for money?" Wendy said. Brian could tell she was trying to act like she disapproved, but she couldn't hide the amusement in her eyes.

Alex put his iPhone away. "The whole world is always scheming for money."

"Pardon me." Max stood right beside Brian, holding a notebook with diagrams and equations all over the page. Over in Wendy's corner, Heather glanced at Brian and Max. She whispered something to Abbie and both of them giggled. "I made some calculations late last night," Max said. "When we meet tonight for the test —"

"Yeah, sure," Brian said quietly. He could feel everybody watching him, thinking he was a nerd like Max. "I've got to . . . sharpen this pencil now." He left Max and went to the sharpener by the door.

Right as he stuck the pencil in, he noticed a woman standing just outside the doorway. She was older than Brian's mother, with flecks of gray sprinkled through her tightly pulled-back dark hair. Her unblinking eyes focused so intensely on him that he imagined she could read his thoughts.

"You must be Brian Roberts," she said. Her words did not sound like a greeting, and her expression was neutral. "I hope you've guessed who I am."

"Yes, Mrs. Gilbert."

The teacher stared at him, raising one eyebrow. "You will address me as *Ms.* Gilbert. Not 'Mrs.' or 'Miss.' I am neither married nor a little girl. Do you understand?"

"Um, yes, Ms. Gilbert." Brian swallowed. Wendy hadn't been kidding about Gilbert being strict.

"Good." Ms. Gilbert's face showed no emotion. "You seem to be the only one who has not yet found a seat. You may sit in the empty desk behind Alex Mackenzie in the second row from the door and the fourth desk back."

Brian nodded and walked back to his seat.

"And Brian?"

He froze just as he was about to sit down.

"Students are not allowed to bring any sort of bag to my classroom, and they are certainly not to bring skateboards. Today, you may keep your bag and skateboard on the counter. You should have been assigned a locker at registration. Tomorrow you will report to the office for your locker number and combination."

Brian felt like a bobble-head doll for nodding so much. He took his seat, grateful to be out of the spotlight, at least for now.

They spent the first hour in Ms. Gilbert's room being lectured about the rules and getting their language arts textbooks. Then they moved on to other subjects, rotating to the classroom of the other sixth grade teacher, Mrs. Brown, as well as the rooms of the fifth grade teachers. All morning they heard more rules. By the time they returned to Ms. Gilbert's classroom, Brian was so tired of rules that he was almost hoping for homework. He killed time by flipping through his language arts textbook, looking for at least one good story.

It was almost noon. The loud noise of the little kids echoed down the hall from the cafeteria. Brian's stomach rumbled, and others kept shifting in their seats around him. Ms. Gilbert stood up at her desk. "When the bell rings for lunch, you will wait in your seats until I dismiss you. You will not stampede down to the cafeteria like animals." She stared at them all for a long quiet moment. The bell rang. Nobody moved. "Good," she said. "You may go to lunch."

Red stood up from his desk. "Alex, where you sitting?"

David slapped Alex on the back. "Hey, let's sit where the sixth grade guys sat last year, farthest away from the cooks and the lunch monitor's desk." The three of them headed down the aisle toward the front of the room.

The cool table, Brian thought. That's where all the action was. All the best jokes and the most fun. At least that was how it had been back in Seattle — for some people, anyway. If you sat at the wrong table with the wrong people, you could end up being made fun of a lot. Brian stood up. He figured he better hurry to catch up with Alex and the guys.

"I believe crispitos are featured on today's menu," Max said from behind him. "They are a sort of crispy beef burrito. They're usually tasty enough, but I don't think they accurately reflect the culture that first —"

"Mad Max!" Red stopped in the doorway on his way out. "Who cares about all that culture stuff? It's crispito day! I'm eating four of those suckers."

"Gross," Heather said.

"Brian," said Max quietly. He kept his eyes fixed on the floor. "I was wondering if you would be interested in sitting with —"

Brian thought fast. "Shoot. You know what?" he said right as they reached the door. "I, um, have to talk to Ms. Gilbert about something."

"Oh. Well, I certainly don't mind waiting for you."

"Oh no." Brian made a motion with his hand as if he was trying to sweep Max into the hallway. "Go on ahead. I don't want to take up your lunchtime."

The wide-eyed, hopeful look in Max's face fell almost as if it were melting. Brian clenched his fists, hoping that Max would just go. "No, seriously," he said. "I think this is going to take a really long time."

"Oh. Well . . . okay." Max left the room and headed down the now empty hallway toward the cafeteria.

Brian waited until Max was out of sight. Max was a good

guy, and it was terrible to lie to him, especially since he was one of only two people here in Iowa he could count as a friend. Still, being friends with a bunch of the fun people in the class or friends with just one guy . . . what would anyone choose?

"Brian?"

Brian jumped and spun around. Ms. Gilbert had switched off the lights in the room and sat reading at her desk by the light of a small lamp. Spooky. "Oh. Um. Ms. Gilbert."

"You're supposed to be at lunch," she said.

He nodded. "I, um, had a question."

She stared at him for a moment. "And what *is* your question?"

His hands were sweaty. "Well, the . . . I was looking through the textbook."

"Is there a question coming sometime?"

"I was wondering, you know . . . if there are any good stories in it." His cheeks felt hot now. He knew he must have been flaring red.

"There's a story from Greek mythology about Daedalus and his son Icarus, who escape a terrible maze by building wings and flying away. Icarus is a fast and daring flyer, and so —"

"That sounds cool." Brian was only half listening. Max should have had time to get through the lunch line and sit down by now. How could he get out of here?

The corner of Ms. Gilbert's mouth curled up into something almost like a smile. "Yes, it most certainly is . . . cool."

There was more quiet. "Now, I think you need to get to lunch. I know I'd certainly like to be left alone to read my book."

She turned her attention back to what she'd been reading, and Brian left for the lunchroom.

A few other kids must have been held up by teachers or had business in the office, because he ended up third from last in line. He got his crispito thing, pears, and milk and went to face the sea of strangers in the crowded cafeteria. He quickly scanned the tables, looking for Alex and Red. Out of the corner of his eye, he noticed Max sitting by himself, trying to wave him down, but Brian pretended he didn't see him.

There was one last empty spot at the table where Alex and the guys sat. Maybe Brian hadn't been invited, but Dad would have said that this was one of those times to take a risk. He picked up his pace toward the other end of the lunchroom. Alex looked up from his tray and tilted his head back in one of those cool sort of reverse nods.

Then something crashed right into Brian and sent his tray flying. His crispito hit the tiles and split open. Pears slid along the floor. People at tables all around him burst out laughing. And Frankie Heller was right there, laughing loudest of all.

"Frankie Heller, what are you doing?" Mrs. Brown stood up from her little table at the far end of the room, back by the lunch counter. She put her hands on her hips and frowned.

"Oh gosh, I'm so sorry." Frankie put a scared look on his face. "I didn't see you there, Brian. Can I get you another tray?" He didn't wait for Brian's answer but leaned closer. "What?" He cupped his hand to his ear. "I can't hear you!" he shouted.

"Why can't you just leave me alone?" Brian said.

Frankie stepped away. "Oh, okay. If you're sure you want to get your own tray." He looked at the teacher. "Sorry about that, Mrs. Brown." He shrugged and went to the guys' table, sitting down in the last seat with a big grin on his face.

Brian looked to Alex, hoping he'd make some room for Brian to join him. Alex caught his gaze for an instant, but then he looked down at his tray. He wasn't going to say or do anything.

Mrs. Brown was beside him. "Don't worry about that mess now," she said. "We're going to run out of time. Just hurry and get another tray."

Brian went back to the lunch counter. He could hear people laughing at him, talking about him — Frankie most of all, with his loud thunder voice, sitting in Brian's seat. Brian picked up a new tray of soggy pears and a cold crispito and went to the empty table right by the lunch counter. He sat down to eat, trying to ignore the fact that he had just been branded a total loser in the eyes of everyone at his new school. That everything was going wrong. That here in Iowa, like here in this cafeteria, he was completely alone.

The afternoon was mostly time for schoolwork. Since they hadn't been assigned much yet, Ms. Gilbert had them read a story out of the language arts textbook, something about a boy who lived in South America and was having trouble getting his fruit to market. Brian found it hard to pay attention.

When the final bell rang for the day, he figured it was best to grab his things and hurry out of the building ahead of the crowd. But instead of going out the front, where everybody could make fun of him about the cafeteria incident and Frankie might pull another stunt, he bolted for the back door. Soon everybody would be gone and he could head home.

After Brian had waited out back for at least ten minutes, Max came out the back door too. He checked his digital calculator watch. "I believe Frankie has left for the day. However, sometimes he lingers in front. If you'd like, I could show you a different way home."

How pathetic was this? Brian wasn't fooling anyone. "Sure. I mean . . . whatever you want."

Max led the way out to the playground behind the school. They went through the pea-gravel pit, past the plastic slides and climbing equipment, on across the baseball field. Brian kept looking out for Alex and the guys, and Frankie. A large oak stood in the corner of the schoolyard, right next to the big wood fence.

"Um, Max, where are we going?"

Max stopped by the tree. "Sometimes when I have experienced a tough day at school and want to get home quickly, I take this shortcut." He went between the thick trunk and the fence, then climbed up to a large branch that reached out over the top of the fence.

"It's like a sort of bridge," Brian said. "A back way out of here."

"Precisely." Max scooted out onto the limb. When he passed over the top of the fence, he dropped down out of sight.

Brian handed his backpack and skateboard over the fence and then climbed up into the tree. He went across and found the branch reached pretty low on the other side. It was an easy jump to the ground, a grass strip near a cornfield.

Max handed Brian his things. "Follow me," he said. He walked off into the field, holding his hands up so that his forearms blocked his face.

Brian followed but didn't protect himself — at least not at first. After the second long cornstalk leaf nailed him in the eye, he held his skateboard up like a shield. They rustled their way through the rows. "How long are we going to have to cut through here?"

"We're almost to the turn."

What turn? Every way Brian looked, all he saw was more corn, six feet high all around him. He kept walking until he bumped right into Max.

"We change direction here." Max started off to the right.

Brian followed. "Wait. How do you know?"

"We're twenty-seven rows in."

"You've been counting?"

Max didn't reply. He had said he took this shortcut home when he'd had a bad day. How many bad days did it take to memorize a secret route through the corn?

When they finally emerged from the field, they had reached the dead end of a street Brian didn't recognize.

"This is Tilford Street." Max took off his glasses and blew dust off the lenses. "You know, your grandfather lives on this street on the other edge of town. We could go to the Eagle's Nest and put in some final checks on the flying machine."

After a rotten mess of a school day, checking out the flyer sounded pretty great. "Sure, let's see what we can get done."

In the Eagle's Nest, Max went to the side of the flyer opposite the tunnel. Brian pulled the cover off it.

"I returned last night after we all left the Eagle's Nest —"

"Whoa, wait a minute. How late were you here? Didn't your parents mind?"

Max tilted his head. "My parents often work late at the university. Even when they're home, they are sometimes so absorbed in their work that they don't notice I've slipped out. It's how I found the time to build the flyer in the first place. Anyway, last night, I didn't need much time because I merely checked to make sure all the controls are working correctly. What do you think?"

The light from the bright bulb hanging over the table gleamed on the flyer's white Plastisteel wings. "She's a beautiful machine, Max."

Max sighed. "You know, in modern practice, vehicles are generally not called by personal pronouns. That is, boats and airplanes are usually 'it' and 'its' rather than 'she' or 'her.'"

"I don't know what you're talking about, but it sounds so *boring*!" Alex emerged from the tunnel holding a bag of Doritos and a pack of cookies in one hand along with a case of Mountain Dew in the other. "Please tell me this isn't a homework party."

"Preflight checks," said Brian.

Max nodded. "We should be ready to fly tonight after dark."

"That's what I'm talking about!" Alex shook his treats above his head. "You guys got to help me with this stuff, though."

"I'm afraid I have no means to keep the soda cold," Max said.

"Have to drink them fast, then." Alex took three sodas out of the box, setting his on the table and giving one to Brian and another to Max before putting the rest on the tool bench. "So what's the plan?"

"I have prepared a detailed presentation about the take-off procedure." Max pulled a big rolled piece of paper out of the drawer beneath the computer, unwound it, and taped it to the wall. It was a giant map of Riverside. He fired his *Star Trek* phaser pointer at the map. "We are here. We will wait until nightfall to move under the cover of darkness." He moved the red dot to the doors. "We'll carry the flyer out the main doors, across the street, around the back of Alex's house, and north up into the fields." The red dot moved up the map and hooked around across a light dotted line for a gravel road. It reached a heavy dotted line. "This is the abandoned railroad." He moved the laser down the rail line. "We'll have to carry the flyer all the way down the tracks across the highway and over the Runaway Bridge."

The laser left the tracks. "Then we carry it off the rails through the woods to the grain elevators. There's a new paved driveway there that should be long and smooth enough for a good takeoff. Additionally, it's secluded, so we should remain unnoticed."

He looked at Brian. "Once you're airborne, you'll need to gain altitude to clear the trees down by the river, then adjust the heading to starboard and fly south to stay out of town. The grain elevators are visible for miles and the American flag is always lighted on top, so you should be able to find your way back to the runway. A streetlight provides illumination on the driveway itself."

"Starboard?" Alex asked.

Max sighed. "The starboard side is the right side."

"'Port' means 'left,'" said Brian.

"Well, why not just *say* 'right' or 'left,' then?"

Brian shrugged. "'Starboard' and 'port' sound way cooler."

"Moreover, the noise of the engine and the wind will be significant, even despite the windshield," Max said. "The monosyllabic words 'right' and 'left' might get mixed up, but 'port' and 'starboard' sound diff —"

"Okay, okay, 'starboard' right, 'port' left. I got it!" Alex took a long drink of his Mountain Dew. "So that's the plan? What else do we need?"

"Just some gasoline," Max said.

"Gas?" Alex asked.

"Yes, Alex," said Max. "This modern internal combustion engine actually runs on gasoline."

Alex shot Max a look that seemed to ask if he was

serious. Brian couldn't tell. Finally, Max's neutral expression cracked and he laughed.

Alex tried to act like Max's joke had insulted him, but he couldn't hide his smile. "Well, I don't know what this thing runs on, Mr. Scientist!" With a bob of his head, he let out a deep, long, vibrating belch, blowing it in Max's face. Max turned away with his T-shirt pulled up over his mouth.

Brian reached out and high-fived Alex. "That was huge," he spoke through his own belch. "But we still have to run preflight checks."

"I checked over the controls last night," said Max.

"Dad never took his Cardinal up without running his own checks," Brian said.

"Are you sure you know how to do all that stuff?" Alex stuffed a handful of Doritos in his mouth.

"You're worried about me doing preflight, but you're just fine with me piloting the flyer?"

Alex spoke the best he could with his mouth full of chips. "Everybody is on my case today!" A few crumbs fell out of his mouth. Max held up the package of cookies and looked questioningly at Alex. "Dude, go ahead," said Alex. "I brought them for you guys."

Brian bent down and saw that Max had wedged pieces of wood in front of and behind the skateboard wheels to keep the flyer from rolling on the table. He climbed up into the pilot's seat, letting his feet rest on the decks of the skateboards.

The small control panel behind the engine had only two levers. On the left was the throttle. He would push it up to increase speed, and pull it down to reduce power. In the center was the control stick, which looked like it had been salvaged from an old video game. He saw that Alex was watching.

"If I pull the yoke back," Brian said, "the horizontal stabilizer flap in the tail goes up, so the tail goes down and the nose rises." He pushed the yoke to the right. The flap at the back of the right-side wing went up, while the flap on the other wing went down. "With the yoke to the right, the starboard aileron goes up while the port side goes down, so the plane rolls to starboard." He watched again to make sure everything was working right. Max had done a great job rigging all the interior cables and pulleys within the wings. "Yoke to the left, the ailerons go the opposite way and the flyer rolls to port."

Brian put his feet on the pedals. He pushed the right one. "Right pedal down moves the tail rudder to the right, turning the aircraft to starboard." It was all working fine. He tested the rudder to port as well. "She checks out, just like a real plane."

"That's because it *is* a real plane," said Max. He pointed to a Plastisteel bar across the span between the skateboards in the back. Attached to the bar were two levers that operated two small, rubber-tipped pieces of metal. "This is the brake system. Upon landing, Alex will have to lower both levers simultaneously to lock the brakes to the ground."

"Those look like little door stoppers."

"That's because they are door stoppers."

Alex held his hands up. "Dude. Seriously."

"If you have a better way of bringing eight skateboard wheels to a stop, please let me know."

Alex made gun hands and dropped his thumbs to shoot Brian and Max. "Okay, you know your stuff. Both of you, actually." He blew on the tips of his fingers like they were smoking.

"She's ready to fly!" Brian stood up on the table, careful not to knock down any of the model planes. "Give me another Mountain Dew!"

Alex tossed him a soda. When Brian opened it, fizz shot out. He put his mouth on it and drank as fast as he could, trying not to laugh like the other two. When the fizz finally stopped, he put his hand to his throat. "Burns from chugging."

"That is your punishment for standing up on top of the table," Max said.

"Yeah," said Alex. "If Gilbert caught you doing that at your desk, she'd revoke your . . . how did she say it?"

"She'd revoke your privilege of having a seat and force you to remain standing for an undetermined period of time," Max said.

Even though Ms. Gilbert was nowhere around and the Eagle's Nest was a total secret, Brian still felt compelled to get down and take a seat at the edge of the table. "What is with that lady anyway?"

Max frowned. "She is rather strict."

They drank more soda and ate more chips and cookies while they joked and complained about school. After a while they agreed to go home for supper, only to return after dark for their first test flight. They really would fly tonight. Brian could hardly wait.

Brian was hoping that supper would be a sandwich on the go so he could get back to the Eagle's Nest. But Dad had made spaghetti and meatballs, his favorite. He'd have to eat quickly, but he still planned to eat a lot.

"Slow down, Brian," Mom said. "What's your hurry? Your father made this nice meal. Enjoy it."

Brian swallowed a large bite of meatball. "Sorry," he said. "It's just so good." He shoveled another meatball into his mouth.

"I mean it, Brian. Slow. Down. How was your first day of school?"

He didn't want to tell them the truth, but he was happy not to have to lie. "Well, I made two new friends so far, these guys Alex and Max." He spun some spaghetti around his fork and ate it quickly. "I was hoping to go hang out with them tonight."

Dad was making notes on one of his spreadsheets. He didn't look up when he spoke. "Max a good guy?"

Brian shrugged. "I guess so. Is that okay, if I go after supper?"

Dad didn't answer. It was quiet. Was he angry? Mom put down her fork and rubbed her eyes, watching Dad writing on his paper.

"Jack? Are you all right?"

Dad shook his head. "What?" He looked up from his figures. "I'm sorry. What did you say?"

Mom sighed. "Jack, couldn't you give work a rest, at least for dinner?"

"I know. I know. I just have to get this one thing worked out before I forget. Things are going . . ." He pressed his lips together tightly and blew out through his nose. "Could have really used that financial help."

"You promised," Mom whispered.

Dad put his pen down. "Fine. I'll just stay up until two in the morning trying to figure out where we're supposed to get money to improve production methods, but that's fine."

Lots of times, adults saying "fine" felt a lot worse than if they just said "everything is terrible." Brian spun a huge clump of spaghetti around his fork and crammed it in his mouth, chewing it as fast as he could. That would round out his second full plate.

"Come on," Mom said. "We were going to have a nice night."

"We are. Just one quick figure was all —"

"Please, Jack. Can we not do this tonight?"

The only thing they didn't seem to argue about was letting Brian go when he asked to be excused.

A half hour later, the boys were carrying the aircraft across town. They stopped by the highway to wait until it was clear, then they rushed across the road and followed the train tracks into the woods near the river. "Can we rest a minute, guys?" Brian asked. "It's really amazingly light, but it's just a little awkward to carry. I feel like I'm going to drop it."

"I concur. Let's take a break," Max said.

"Yeah," Alex said. "Right here on the Runaway Bridge."

They had reached the middle of a big bridge made of giant blocks of limestone. The tracks ran down the middle, with small scrub grass growing up between the wooden ties and three feet of stone on either side of the steel rails. The sound of water churning around the center support column came from far below. Brian walked over to the edge to take a look. There was no side barrier, nothing to keep them from falling off. More than fifty feet down, moonlight sparkled on the water of the English River.

"Brian, be careful." Max was crouched down next to him.

"Are you kidding me?" Brian said. "I'm about to fly an experimental aircraft. Maybe she'll hold together. Maybe not. But this bridge has been here for a hundred years or whatever. I think I'm okay."

"Still," said Alex. "You don't have to stand that close to the edge."

Brian smiled. How could people be afraid of heights when they were perfectly safe? "Is that why they call this the Runaway Bridge, because everybody is so scared to be on it?"

"Whatever, dude," Alex said. "Just if you fall, you won't be able to help us carry the flyer back to the Nest."

"I think it would be a good idea to keep going. Let's get the flyer into position for takeoff," Max said.

If it was a challenge to carry the flyer all the way down the railroad tracks and across the bridge, it was even tougher to get it down the embankment and through the woods. The weeds and shrubs kept snagging the wings, skateboards, or tail assembly.

"Perhaps it would have been a good idea to come here earlier to clear brush and prepare a path for the flyer," Max said. Sweat beaded on his forehead.

"Yeah, no joke. This is the worst runway taxi I've ever seen," Brian said.

Finally, they cleared the woods at the edge of the grain elevator's lot and brought the flyer around to the blacktop lane. They set it down in takeoff position with its nose pointed straight down the center of the long flat stretch of pavement.

Brian stretched his arms and drew in a deep breath. For the last week of August, the air was cool and still. A great night to fly. He looked up. Beyond the tops of the tall, skinny evergreen trees that lined both sides of the driveway, the open sky and the stars seemed to call to him.

"Let's do this," he said. "Let's fly!"

"Yeah!" Alex rushed to the backseat, but before he sat down, he stopped and motioned toward Brian's chair. "You're the pilot. You should board first."

Brian grinned too, approaching the flyer. "She looks great."

"Yeah, it does," Alex said.

Brian slapped him a high five. "She's ready." He sat down. Alex took his seat next. "We're ready."

"If you don't mind, I'd like to start the engine," Max said. Brian waved toward the handle on the pull start. Max took hold of the handle. "When the engine starts, gently push the throttle lever up to give it more power."

"Woo-hoo!" Alex shouted. "Let's go!"

Max laughed. "Prepare to engage engine." He yanked the starter cable. The engine rumbled a little, but didn't fire up. He frowned and pulled harder. This time the engine sputtered and popped for a moment, then the propeller began to spin and the engine roared to life. Max backed away and gave them the thumbs-up.

They were rolling! Slowly, maybe, but the flyer was moving under its own power with the propeller pulling them forward. Brian eased the throttle up, giving the engine more gas to increase speed.

Alex tapped him on the shoulder. Brian risked a look back. Alex grinned widely as he leaned forward. "It's working! It's really working!"

Brian pushed the lever the rest of the way up. "Full throttle!"

The flyer moved fast now. Brian was pushed back in his seat. He loved this part. The thrill of the aircraft's power. The mad rush just before takeoff. Speeding up to the skies.

They were halfway down the runway. Brian pulled back on the yoke. The nose lifted. The front wheels were off the ground! The back wheels were up next. "We're flying!" he shouted. "I can't believe it! We're really flying!"

But even though the yoke was back, the plane came down and hit the pavement again. It rolled a bit farther and went up for a few seconds more before falling again. Brian cranked the yoke harder. Maybe he wasn't pulling enough.

Maybe the cables controlling the horizontal stabilizer weren't engaging right.

"What's up?" Alex shouted over the noise from the wind and engine.

"Not us," Brian answered. "Not yet." He gripped the yoke, pulling with all his weight. They were up now, two, maybe three feet off the ground.

"Dude, this is awesome! We're flying!" Alex said. "You got it!"

No, I don't, Brian thought. The pitch wasn't right. The nose should be pointing higher when he had the yoke pulled all the way back. Instead they were level. The flyer smacked back down on its wheels.

"Give it some gas!"

"She's at full throttle already!" The flyer was up and then down again. This was bad. They were running out of runway! They needed to get more air right now. He'd have to bank her hard as soon as they were off the ground, then shoot right down the highway to avoid hitting the trees on the other side of the road.

Brian shoved the yoke all the way forward and then pulled it back. Twenty feet of runway left. They went up — maybe four feet this time — then down again. They were going to roll right across the highway. Brian pulled the throttle lever all the way back to power down. He hit the kill switch to shut off the engine.

"The road!" Alex shouted. "I'll hit the brakes!"

"No, don't!" Brian called back. "You'll stop us right in the middle of the highway. Just hold on!"

"Of course I'm holding on!" Alex screamed. "The heck you think I'm doing?"

"Please no cars, please no cars, no cars, no cars, no cars," Brian whispered. The flyer rolled out into the highway. A pair of headlights made his stomach leap in terror for a moment until he realized they were over a mile away. The flyer hit the gravel on the shoulder of the far side, and as the ground below them dropped away into a deep, grassy ditch, they glided out into the air. They cleared the barbed-wire fence below and sailed into the woods. Twigs from a low branch whapped Brian in the face, scratching his cheek.

"Ow!" Alex shouted. The branch must have hit him too.

A huge tree trunk was dead ahead. Brian steered the flyer's nose clear to port just in time, but the starboard wing cracked hard against the trunk. He lurched forward as they spun flat and hard to the right. Then he was thrown back in his seat when the flyer slopped down into the mud.

It was quiet except for a tick in the engine and the gurgle of the English River nearby. Brian touched his cheek. It was already swollen, and his fingers came away wet and sticky with blood.

"Brian?" Alex said. "You okay?"

"I'm fine. Not so sure about the flyer, though." Brian stood up. His foot sank down in thick mud. "Or my shoes."

"Brian? Alex?" Max appeared up on the road, silhouetted by the weak light filtering in from the streetlight across the road. "Have you sustained any injuries?"

"Have we sustained . . . Why can't he talk normal for once?" Alex said quietly to Brian. Then he called back, "We're okay, even though your flyer almost got us killed!"

Max stumbled down into the brush to meet them. "I'm very sorry. I followed the wing and tail design specifications for conventional aircraft. Plastisteel is lighter. The takeoff should have worked. I don't understand what went wrong."

"What went wrong is that I never should have agreed to this in the first place," said Alex. "If it hadn't been for Brian, we would have hit that tree head-on."

"It's not that bad," Brian said. "What *really* went wrong, Max, is that the wings, tail, and propeller might be in the style of other planes, but this has to be the first flyer with skateboard landing gear. Skateboard wheels are light and can handle speed, but there are still eight of them. That's a lot of drag to overcome."

Max leaned over the flyer, checking for damage. "Fortunately, the engine is intact. I'll have to find a way to improve it, to give the flyer enough power to overcome the drag."

"Yeah, well, you'll have to do it without me. I'm out of here." Alex started walking away.

"Alex, wait," Brian said. "We were flying! We must have been four feet up for a while. I thought we were really going to take off."

"You thought wrong."

Brian couldn't let this fall apart. Working with these two on the flyer was the best part about living in Iowa. "So you're just going to give up?" he said. "What about the money we're going to make?"

Alex stopped. "Nobody wants to pay for an interview with three guys who made a plane that *almost* flew."

"Nobody wants to buy the story of three kids who succeeded on the first try! People always want to hear about overcoming difficulties and crap like that. This will just make our story better, more valuable. We'll fix her! It won't be that hard."

"Actually, it will mostly involve repairs to the starboard wing," said Max, who was crouched in the dark by the flyer.

Brian bent down and examined the right wing by touch. He did not like what he felt. There was a dent right in the forward section of the wing, with a crack running back from the middle of it.

"It's not that bad," he said. "Plastisteel has to be the strongest stuff on earth. We nailed that tree and the wing has just this tiny dent. We can fix this no problem." Brian hoped he sounded believable enough to convince Alex to stay.

Alex squelched through the mud back toward them. "You really think it will be that easy?"

Max stood up. "Unfortunately —"

Brian elbowed Max. "Unfortunately, we're going to have to lift her up out of the mud and carry her back to the Eagle's

Nest tonight. Then, yeah, you and I will fix up the wing real quick, while Max works on improving the engine. We'll be flying in, what . . . a week or so?"

"Actually —" said Max.

"We actually will," Brian said quickly. "Hey, Alex, do you think you would be able to set up the interviews and stuff soon after that? Or maybe it's too hard on short notice, and we should just wait until after winter when we can fly again."

"Are you kidding?" Alex said. "The publicity and the money is the easy part as long as we can get this thing flying."

"We can make it fly," Max said.

"If we promise that we all stay with the project," said Brian.

There was a little silence.

"Okay," said Alex.

They carried the broken flyer back to the Eagle's Nest, but they were so tired by the time they got there that nobody wanted to do anything besides call it a night.

Brian walked home. He gently eased the back door open and slipped inside, holding his muddy shoes in his free hand. His filthy jeans were rolled up so they wouldn't get dirt all over the floor.

In the kitchen, only the little light above the stove was on. The house was silent. He peeked around the corner to the living room to see if Mom was reading in her favorite chair. She must have gone to bed early. She sometimes did that back in Seattle after big arguments.

Brian walked softly through the living room, careful to keep quiet on the wood floor by stepping first onto his bare heel, and then rolling forward onto his toes. Light spilled out from under the door to Dad's office. He was still up working. He was always working.

Why did he even bother sneaking around? Nobody ever noticed him anyway. They probably wouldn't even care about the cut and bruise on his cheek. He almost wished he would get in trouble for it.

He half smiled at the thought. The crash must have scrambled his brains.

After washing off the muck in the shower, which stung his scraped face, Brian dressed for bed and lay down on top of his bedspread in the dark, his hands behind his head on his pillow. A little light from the streetlamp on the corner reached inside his room, while the leaves on the tree outside made creepy shadows on the wall. Exhausted from the night's adventure, Brian fell asleep at once.

The next morning, Brian stood on the deck of the half-pipe at the park, his back wheels over the edge and his front wheels up. He stomped the front of his board and dropped hard into the ramp. Down across the flat bottom, up the far transition to the lip on the other deck. He kicked his board up to grind his trucks on the lip before throwing the front of the board back into the ramp and up to where he had started.

Brian let out a long breath with his eyes closed, feeling the morning sun shine on his face. After the trouble yesterday with Frankie Heller and the flyer that wouldn't fly, he needed something to go right, so he'd left the house extra early to skate it out with *Spitfire*. One of these days he would get enough air to hit the full 360-degree airborne spin. He was close. He knew it.

He also knew that it was a long skate to school, a lot of it uphill, and if he didn't get going, he'd be late. Somehow he doubted Ms. Gilbert appreciated tardiness. He rolled out of the skate park and up Weigand Street past the square, moving fast and jumping curbs. Then he kicked like mad until he reached Lincoln Street at the top of the hill. Here, he could relax a little and enjoy the smooth run on the gentle downward slope until the hill dropped steeply near the school.

As he cleared the intersection at Seventh Street, he almost lost his balance. Wendy whipped around the corner onto Lincoln on her own board.

"Woo-hoo! Come on, Brian! Keep up!" She looked back at him.

She was a block ahead of him already. Brian kicked the pavement hard to go faster, Wendy coasting so he could join her.

"Wow, that hill is a rush!" she said as he came up alongside her. She knocked on her purple helmet. "Glad I'm wearing this."

As they approached school, she jumped off her board and jogged to a stop, kicking up her board to carry it as she walked. Brian did the same. She frowned when she saw the bruise and scrape on his face. "What happened?"

"Oh, this?" Brian touched his injury. "I, um . . . I fell down."

"And landed on your face?"

They both heard the rumble of skateboard on pavement getting louder and louder behind them. Frankie was skating up on a fast approach. Brian gripped *Spitfire*'s truck. He could use his board as a club if Frankie wanted a fight.

Instead, the tough guy just rolled right past them. His eyes were cold and hateful as he stared at Brian, his fists tightly clenched. Frankie might try to hide the mean things he did from his sister, but Brian knew there would be trouble with him later.

"Forget him," Wendy said after a moment. "Come on." Her hand gently touched Brian's elbow, and a tingling shiver went all through him. They walked together in silence for a while, then Wendy finally spoke. "I'm sorry my brother is acting like this. I know you don't believe me, but he really is a good guy. He's just having a tough time with . . ." Her voice trailed off.

With being a jerk? With threatening people? With making Brian miserable? "What?" he said.

"Nothing," said Wendy. She took off her helmet and ran her fingers through her long dark hair. She looked at him. Her eyes were such a deep green. "It's like lately he's always looking for trouble. Just promise me you won't fight him?"

Sure, Brian could agree not to fight Frankie — but what if Frankie fought him? It didn't matter. Wendy looked so sad, he couldn't help but agree. "Sure," he said. "I promise."

She smiled and looked like she was about to say something, but instead she just gave Brian a slow-motion punch to the shoulder. "Thank you." She went inside, where she was immediately snatched away by the Wolf Pack.

Brian couldn't stop thinking about Wendy as he stopped by the office and picked up his locker information. Her face was still in his mind as he struggled to open his new locker. Max stood three lockers away.

Then an elbow crunched into Brian's back and his face slammed into his locker. Frankie spoke in almost a growl right near his ear. "Twelve minutes. That's how long it took you and my sister to get here this morning. Figure fifteen from yesterday. And I'm going to make you pay for every minute of it." He chuckled. Brian wanted to shove him away or punch him, but Frankie had his arm gripped tight around Brian's shoulders like they were buddies. "This little locker slam was good for one minute." He gave Brian a quick, hard slap to the face. "That's another. Thirty minutes to go."

That wasn't right. "Twenty . . . Twenty-six," Brian said.

"Well, golly," Frankie said in an exaggerated hick tone. "I guess you're right. I ain't never been no good at figuring them there numbers." He started walking away, but stopped long enough to crush Max up against the lockers, his hand gripping Max's shirt. "Sorry I haven't been around to thump on you in a few days, Mad Max. I've been busy with this new guy." He grinned. "I'll get to you soon, though. I promise."

Brian put his skateboard and backpack in the locker and acted like he was shuffling around on the shelf for some books. He heard people laughing, but when he sneaked a peek, David, Red, and even Jess O'Claire just looked away, snickering and whispering to one another.

The morning classes went the same as the day before, except the teachers started up with lessons and homework. At midday, while everyone else charged to the lunchroom when Ms. Gilbert dismissed them, Brian held back.

"Are you heading to the cafeteria, Brian?" Max said quietly from the desk behind his as the last of their classmates left the room.

"Um . . ." Brian started. He should just go to lunch with Max. Max was a good guy. But Frankie had been taking every chance he could to hurt or humiliate him, and he couldn't stand giving him more ammunition by hanging around with Max. "Oh, go ahead. I'm going to take too long. I . . . um . . . have to organize this . . . thing in my desk. Then I have to ask Ms. Gilbert something."

Max frowned. "Are you sure? I'm happy to —"

"No, really. Go ahead."

Max looked at him for just a moment and then lowered his gaze to the floor as he walked out. Brian sighed and shook his head.

Since Tuesday's homework load was extreme, Max insisted on going home after school. Brian and Alex figured there wasn't much point in trying to work on the flyer by themselves, so they all agreed to meet the next day.

At lunchtime on Wednesday, Brian didn't have to make up any lame excuses to avoid Max. He really did have to go to the bathroom. The only problem was that Frankie found him at the urinal. He pushed Brian in the back and made him pee all over himself.

"About twenty-eight minutes left to pay for!" Frankie laughed on his way out of the bathroom.

Brian missed all of lunch trying to splash water from the sink onto his pants to wash the pee off. This made an even bigger wet spot, so then he had to stand there for a long time with his crotch under the hand drier.

Timmy Hale, from the other sixth grade classroom, came into the bathroom.

"I spilled ketchup in my lap," Brian lied.

"Whatever," said Timmy. He did his business, washed his hands, and left quickly, laughing as he sneaked a look at Brian on the way out. Brian wanted to get back at Frankie somehow, but he had promised Grandpa that he would stay out of trouble and Wendy that he would not fight her brother.

He skated home slowly that afternoon, dumping his book bag on the floor in the entryway. The house was empty and silent. A note on the fridge told him that both Mom and Dad would be working late. He was supposed to go to Grandpa's house for supper at seven. Brian sighed. He wasn't ready for all of Grandpa's questions about school. Grabbing his skateboard and heading for the door, Brian figured he'd check in at the Eagle's Nest first to delay the visit with Grandpa and see if the flyer could be salvaged.

When Brian came up out of the tunnel, Alex and Max were standing at the table in the center. A math book was open in front of them. "I hate story problems!" Alex was saying. "Why doesn't stupid Miguel just sell lemonade made from a cheap mix or yellow food coloring or something? He'd make a lot more money for half the work that way. But no! He's got to squeeze fresh lemons, and now I'm supposed to figure out how many lemons he'd need if he wants to expand his business?" He slammed the math book closed and pointed at the cover as he shouted, "Stop riding trains from New York to San Francisco and figuring out how large the pizza slices should be and how many lemons you need for your stupid lemonade stand! Why don't you just go play video games or something, Miguel? Solve your own problems!"

Max chuckled. "I sympathize with your frustration, but do you understand how to finish the math assignment now?"

"Yeah," Alex said. "I can handle basic math, enough to keep track of how much money people owe me, but these problems drive me nuts. You're a bit strange sometimes, Max, but you're awesome at this stuff."

"I don't know what's worse, the story problems or the super-cheerful way Mrs. Brown explains them," Brian said. He put on a huge grin and opened his eyes as wide as he could. "Okay, boys and girls," he said in a breathy, high-pitched voice. "Today we're going to have fun with fractions!"

Alex and Max laughed. "That's her, dude," Alex said. "Sometimes I want to throw something across the room just to make her mad and get that fake, pasted-on smile off her face for a little while."

"It is a bit disconcerting," Max said.

Brian nodded toward the flyer. "How bad is she?"

"Not as bad as one might expect from a crash of this nature," Max said. "If this had been a standard aluminum airplane, the damage from the collision with the tree would likely have been far more extensive."

"This Plastisteel stuff really rocks." Alex switched on the spotlight above the table. The forward, curved section of the right wing was dented in about three inches. A nasty crack ran back about four inches from the dent.

Brian slid his fingers along the tear. "Sorry about this. I tried to steer us around the tree trunk."

"Don't apologize," Alex said. "You probably saved our lives. If we would have hit that tree head-on . . ."

"Alex is correct," Max said. "Furthermore, you saved the engine."

Alex winced. "Max, don't use the word 'furthermore.' You're not writing a paper for class."

Max ignored him. "It was still excellent flying, Brian."

Brian looked at the dent closely. "Can we just take off the top panel of the wing and then hit the dent from the inside, like with a hammer or something? If hitting it from the outside pushed the Plastisteel in like this, maybe hitting it from the inside would push it back out."

Max shot his phaser pointer along the tear. "Your approach to repairing the dent might work, but this tear presents a more difficult problem."

"Can we just put in a different panel?" Brian asked.

"I don't have any more Plastisteel, so I'd prefer to align it on both sides of the tear as evenly as possible. Then maybe we could find a very strong glue to seal it up."

"We could file it down to make sure it's smooth," said Brian. "The wing would be mostly okay then."

"After that . . ." Alex said. "I don't know. Maybe we could ask Miguel how to get it to fly."

Brian laughed a little, but Max frowned. "The answer to our story problem is a bit more problematic." He took off his glasses and chewed the earpiece.

"But it did fly," Brian said.

"Yeah," said Alex. "It glided for a while down off the highway until it crashed, but —"

"No, I mean on the runway." Brian put his hand on one of the flyer's wings. "She was flying for a little bit. She'd get up two, three, maybe four feet in the air at a time."

Alex nodded. "Then it dropped right back down onto its skateboards. Maybe that's the problem. Are there other wheels we could be using?"

"Other wheels I investigated were too large, too heavy, or couldn't roll fast enough," Max said. "Yet that's still the problem. The flyer needs to move faster in order to overcome the drag created by all those wheels."

Brian pointed to the rocket on the workbench by the wall, labeled the NX-03. "Why don't we just mount that rocket on the flyer?"

"You have a rocket?" Alex asked.

"It's how we got away when Frankie was chasing me at the skate park."

"I was wondering about that. You turned the corner and we couldn't see you through the trees." Alex said. "So that's what that loud noise was."

"I don't think the rocket method will work," Max said. "The NX-02 exploded shortly after its first use."

"Exploded?" said Alex.

Brian spread his hands out to mime the burst.

"We shouldn't use it," said Max. "Even if I could engineer it correctly so it doesn't explode, it is important to consider the physics of a solid-fuel rocket. Once ignited, it will continue to increase speed along one straight line, making it difficult to maneuver the flyer. The best course of action is for me to improve the engine somehow. I'll have to find a way to increase its power so the flyer can move fast enough to take off."

"There it is," Brian said. "You can take the engine apart

and figure that out. Alex and I can get to work fixing the wing."

Nobody said anything for a moment. Max stared at the engine like he had never seen it before. Alex wore a similar expression.

"Guys, don't worry," said Brian. "This is going to work."

"You're right." Alex smiled the way Dad had with Mrs. Douglas. "We're still going to make a pile of money on this. I'd bet on it, and I never lose a bet. Plus —" He reached down into his backpack and pulled out a bag of Oreos, another twelve-pack of Mountain Dew, and a cool set of iPod speakers. "I brought treats and tunes. It may take some work to get this plane flying, but there's no reason we can't have fun in the process."

They each grabbed a couple cookies and cracked open a soda. Then Max busied himself opening up the engine to check on its interior, and Brian and Alex set to work carefully unbolting the wing. Alex put on some music. "I know this song is kind of old, but it's really cool," he said. "The band has a different song that sounds kind of like this. We'll hear that next."

Brian tried to concentrate on unscrewing the Plastisteel on the wing, but he couldn't help thinking that *every* song this band made sounded exactly the same. How did all the popular kids always know which terrible songs were the coolest ones? Why was it weird to like older stuff like the Beatles?

What was so weird about him that made him unable to care very much about whatever was new and popular?

"Dude, you okay?" Alex asked Brian.

"Yeah," said Brian. "Fine. Just . . . listening to this awesome song."

All day Friday, David, Red, Alex, and most of the other guys couldn't stop talking about that night's high school football game. "You going to the game?" was the question of the day. Even the Wolf Pack seemed excited. Once in the hall between classes, Brian could hear their giggly whispers about who they hoped to see at the game and what they would wear. It seemed like only a real loser would skip the game.

So as the band took the field with a marching tune at the end of the first half, with the Dysart Trojans killing the Riverside Roughriders twenty-one to six, Brian found himself sitting on a small corner of Abbie Sark's blanket on the grassy hill by the football field. He wasn't even completely on the blanket — more like half on one corner of it. Still, that was better than Max, who sat off to the side in the grass. Wendy was sitting on the other side of Heather, Abbie, Jess, and Rowena. The only other guys sitting down were Alex, David, and Kevin Stein, who had Mrs. Brown for homeroom. The rest of the boys were out on the practice field, playing football. That was fine by Brian. Frankie could stay with them.

"They'll figure out a better defense during halftime," David said. "Don't count us out yet."

Alex keyed some figures into his iPhone, probably game statistics for other bets. "Yep. Maybe." He looked up and slipped his phone into his pocket. "Even a sure bet's not sure until the game's over."

The Wolf Pack stood up, all except Wendy. They whispered something as they huddled close together, then Jess O'Claire pushed Rowena Stewart out of the circle.

"Come on," Rowena whispered back toward them. They motioned her forward. She shuffled up to the guys, fidgeting with the crystal pendant she always wore. "Um, Kevin." She giggled like someone had just told a joke. Her cheeks were as red as her hair. "Um . . . so Jess was wondering if you want to come with us to the concession stand." Kevin turned toward Alex and David, rolling his eyes. Rowena chewed her thumbnail. "So, do you wanna?"

Kevin sighed. "I guess. You guys coming along?"

Alex stretched out and yawned. "Sure. Why not?" He stood up, along with Kevin and David. Brian started to get to his feet as well.

"Oh, hey," Kevin said to him. "Would it be cool if you two just stayed here? You know, to save our places and stuff."

What did he mean by "you two"? Brian glanced behind him. Max looked like he wanted to go along with the group as well. No wonder Kevin had told them to stay.

"We'll be quick anyway," Alex said.

Brian picked a blade of grass and twisted it in his fingers as he watched David, Kevin, and Alex leave him behind as they headed off with the Wolf Pack. He was left out of the group again.

Then Wendy slid over next to him and he forgot about the other guys. He was sitting, almost alone, on a blanket with Wendy Heller. She wore faded, torn jeans with a couple of paint splatters, along with an ancient Riverside Roughriders T-shirt. "I know it's pretty warm out, but one thing I love about football games is hot chocolate. I was going to go get some." Her face shone in the glow from the lights on the field. He could smell her sweet perfume. "You want to go with?"

She could have asked if he wanted to go with her into a fiery pit full of radioactive poisonous cobras, and he would have gladly followed along. Still, "Why didn't you go with them?" Brian asked, jerking a thumb in the direction the Wolf Pack had taken.

"Ugh." Wendy put her head down, whipping her long hair forward over her face as if to hide. "I have to get away from them for a little bit. All night, Jess has been blathering on about Kevin Stein. Heather was supposed to ask him to go out with her, but Heather won't do it, so now Rowena's going to ask instead." She flipped her hair back and looked at him. "It's like I don't get them sometimes, you know?"

Brian wasn't sure exactly what she meant, but he did know all about not understanding the ways of the Wolf Pack. He nodded.

"Anyway," she said. "You want to go get something?"

"Sure," Brian said. He and Wendy stood up. Max began to move too. "Hey, Max. Yeah, can you stay here and guard the blanket for us?" he said. Wendy had already started toward the refreshment stand. "Just . . . We won't be gone long."

Brian headed off after Wendy. He didn't look back. He didn't want to see Max left there all alone.

On the way to the line for treats, he desperately wanted to say something cool or funny, anything to impress this girl. What would a guy like Alex say? Something about the game. "Too bad the Roughriders aren't doing better."

Wendy shrugged. "Yeah."

That didn't work. What would Red say? Something really bold. David would only talk about the game more. Max? Wendy probably wasn't interested in boring science stuff. He wanted to scream with frustration for not knowing how to talk to this beautiful girl. "You look so . . ." He couldn't just flat out tell her she was pretty. "That's a cool shirt."

Wendy looked pleased. "Thanks."

Finally, they reached the concession stand. "Two hot chocolates, please," Brian said. It felt almost like a date, with him buying something for her. What would a really cool guy do now? "You want anything else?" he offered.

A woman came back to the counter with their two drinks. Her grin was sickeningly big. "That'll be one dollar, kids."

Brian had noticed that anything an adult said that ended with the word "kids" was almost always gushed out in a high-pitched cutesy voice normally used on puppies. This woman was no exception. He reached into his pocket for his money and froze when he realized that all he had left was one dollar. He had just asked Wendy if she wanted something else, and he didn't have a nickel to pay for it.

"Just the hot chocolate is fine, thanks," Wendy said.

He let out a little breath of relief as he slid his dollar over the counter, then took the drinks and handed one to Wendy.

"Thank you." She smiled. "I'll buy next time."

Did that mean there would be a next time? Brian grinned at the thought, even as the first sip of scalding hot cocoa burned his tongue. They walked slowly on the way back to let their steaming drinks cool.

"I love football Fridays," Wendy said after a long quiet. "I don't even really care who wins. I hardly watch the game. It's just fun to hang out with friends, you know?"

"Yeah," he said. Who was she talking about? Did she mean the Wolf Pack or was she talking about him? He hoped she was talking about the girls so maybe he could be more than friends with Wendy. Hadn't she asked him to walk with her to the treat stand? It probably didn't mean anything, but he thought he might actually have a chance with her as long as he didn't do anything too stupid.

"Brian! Catch!"

A football slammed into his hot chocolate, crushing the foam cup and thumping him in the chest. The hot liquid splashed all over his chest and hands. It didn't quite burn him, but his shirt was soaked. Brian waved his hands to cool them.

"Are you okay?" Wendy tried brushing the cocoa off Brian's chest and arms. She spun around and shouted, "Knock it off, Frankie!"

Frankie laughed. He shouted to the guys, "Did you see that? Nailed the cup! Awesome!"

"Why do you have to be such an idiot?" Wendy yelled.

"I said 'catch'!" Frankie said. "It's not my fault he's so clumsy!"

"I think I better go home and get cleaned up," Brian said. So much for not doing anything too stupid.

Wendy followed him toward the gate by the school. "Brian, I'm so sorry."

"It's not your fault," Brian said. They were away from the lights of the field, in the shadows closer to the high school.

"I wish you didn't have to go," she said.

Maybe it was the pain in his hands, his anger over yet another humiliating incident with Frankie, or the disappointment of a great night being ruined, but Brian didn't think about what he said. He just said what was on his mind. "Why?"

"Why don't I want . . ." Wendy twirled a lock of hair around her finger. "I just . . . You're not like all the others, and I think . . . Just . . . I'm sorry about the cocoa. Have a good night, okay?"

"Yeah," he said. "You too."

Brian walked home, more confused than he'd been in a long time.

A week later, Alex, Brian, and Max were in the hayloft in Brian's grandfather's barn. Alex swooped out on the rope.

"You know, we actually have a lot of work to do," Max said as he sat down on a bale. "I thought you said you knew where we could find some more steel cable."

When Brian and Alex had opened the flyer's starboard wing, they found that one of the pulleys inside was damaged. Worse, the cable that operated the aileron had been cut when the wing tore.

"Relax. We'll get the cables." Alex swung in for a skidding landing on the hay. "Brian's grandpa tore down an old building a long time ago, and he saved a whole garage-door kit somewhere in the back of the barn. I remember seeing a bunch of cables and stuff."

"We can't go through the barn without taking a time-out to swing," Brian said. "Come on and try this for once."

Alex flopped down on his back on the hay, laughing. "Yeah, right. Mad Max would never get on the rope like that."

Max closed his eyes and took a deep breath. Brian was pretty sure he didn't appreciate being called Mad Max. "I just think we should concentrate on repairs," Max said.

"Max, come on," Brian said. "It took forever to figure out how to pull the broken cable out of the flyer, and now we have the whole front part of the wing and the cable and pulley system to reconstruct. We deserve a break." He held the rope out toward Max. He wanted Max to swing, not just for the fun of it, but also to do something completely un–Mad Max. "Just try this once."

Max stood up and folded his arms over his chest. "If I swing one time, can we go find those cables and then return to the Eagle's Nest?"

"I promise," Brian said.

"Oh yeah, man!" Alex said. Max took the rope from Brian. Alex sat up. "This I gotta see. It's about time you had some fun, Max."

Max took off his glasses and handed them to Brian. He shook his head, took a deep breath, and then ran out to leap off the bales, gliding out into the open space below. Unlike Brian and Alex who kicked their legs at the far reach of the swing, Max wrapped his legs around the rope. He didn't shout either, but simply swung back and landed on the hay.

He took his glasses back and put them on. "Now, can we please get the hardware the flyer requires and then return to our repair efforts?"

Brian held out a hand to help Alex up. "A deal's a deal."

"I just can't believe we finally got him to try it. Welcome to the club." Alex lightly slapped Max on the back. "That wasn't bad for your first try."

Max led the way down the ladder to the floor of the barn. "I fail to understand why these sorts of initiation rituals always have to involve some sort of risky physical stunt."

"Risky like flying an experimental aircraft?" Alex asked.

Brian laughed out loud at that.

"I mean, who decided the only way to be cool is to swing on a rope like this or do a skateboard jump?" Max said. "Why doesn't anyone ever say, 'Prove you're one of us by solving this complex mathematical equation,' or 'All the cool kids know the atomic weight of plutonium'? Why doesn't anyone ever say, 'Wow, that is so awesome that you understand the entire warp propulsion system for the U.S.S. *Enterprise NCC-1701-D* from *Star Trek: The Next Generation*'?"

Brian couldn't figure out why people thought *Star Trek* was uncool. It was an awesome show. But he also wasn't surprised when Alex shot him a look that said, *This guy is such a nerd*.

"I don't know," Brian said. "But that was a good swing."

"Yeah," Alex said. "That was really cool, man."

Max didn't say anything else, but Brian swore he caught just the hint of a smile.

They skipped that night's football game, spending the whole afternoon and evening opening up more of the wing to get the new pulley and cable in place. The trickiest part was hooking the cable from the aileron to the yoke. Brian couldn't quite get his hands in the small space to make the connections.

They met again the next day to keep working. Brian squeezed the pliers so tightly his hands shook, trying to attach the cable to the yoke mechanism. Finally, he let go. "That should do it. Pull it," he said to Alex.

The yoke moved to the left when Alex pulled the cable. "Seems secure."

Brian wiped the sweat from his brow. "Now we just have to attach the other end to the aileron and then we can start to close it back up."

"Chips first," said Alex, reaching for the Doritos.

"Chips first," Brian said.

Alex and Brian both took a handful. Max watched them from behind the engine, or rather from behind the pile of parts that used to be an engine before he had disassembled it. He had pored over diagrams in a dozen different books and from a bunch of websites, trying to determine how to improve its efficiency and speed, but it looked like he hadn't gotten anywhere yet.

"Doritos, Max?" Brian asked.

"No, thank you. I'm quite busy and my hands are covered in engine oil."

Alex climbed up on the table. "Then I'll just pour some in your mouth. You won't need to use your hands at all."

"No, thank you. I'd really rather not."

"Dude, I'm pouring these out whether or not you eat 'em. They'll get into your engine if you don't open wide right . . ."

Max groaned but put his head under the bag as Alex shook some chips into his mouth. "Shgoo," he said. Pieces of chips fell out of his mouth. "'Sgood," he said. Then he burst out with a laugh and bits of chips flew everywhere.

They all laughed. Alex picked out a single chip with just his orange fingertips. "You are a pig, Mr. Warrender." He chomped down on the lone Dorito. Everyone laughed again.

Brian heard a buzzing sound. Alex wiped his hands on his pants, pulled his phone out of his pocket, and checked the screen before he started typing something back.

"To whom are you sending a text message?" Max asked.

"Hang on." Alex kept pressing the screen. "There," he said. "Just had to answer."

Brian wished he had a phone. Then maybe he would get texts too. "Who texted you?"

"Oh, nobody. Just Red." Alex checked the cable connection to the rudder. Then he went to the engine and looked over all the pieces, nodding as if confirming they were all still there. "Hey, you know what, guys?" He slapped his forehead. "I totally forgot. My parents . . . they have this thing . . . like, a dinner thing, and I have to go."

"Right now?" Brian said.

Max's face was completely emotionless. "On a Saturday afternoon?"

Alex checked his phone again. "Yeah . . ." he said slowly, obviously reading another text. "Well, not right now. But it's a big dress-up thing with their friends."

Max checked his calculator watch. "It's only two forty-five."

"Yeah, I know." Alex headed for the tunnel. "I have to start getting ready. This is going to be so lame. Like wearing a tie. My sister Katie will be in some dumb dress." He crawled down into the tunnel. "Well, awesome work today. Check you later."

When he was gone, Brian and Max stared at the tunnel for a moment. Max had the same look on his face that he wore whenever Brian made up a pathetic excuse to ditch him at lunch.

"I'm glad I don't have to go to some lame dinner with my parents' friends." Brian forced a little laugh. "He probably feels like a total loser right now, don't you think?"

Max didn't answer.

The next Wednesday, Brian came home after working in the Eagle's Nest. As usual, he went to the fridge to find something to eat. He wondered if either of his parents would be home for dinner tonight. Since their arrival in Riverside, Dad had worked late in Iowa City with Dr. Warrender most evenings, while just Brian and Mom had supper. Those beat the nights Dad worked into the night *and* Mom had to stay late at the office. Then Brian just had microwaved leftovers or made a sandwich.

"Hey, buddy," Dad said behind him. Brian jumped and spun around. Dad held his hands up. "Whoa. Sorry. I didn't mean to startle you. Where were you this afternoon?"

"Nowhere." He backed up against the fridge. "Hanging out with Alex and Max."

"Mom is working late, so it's just you and me for supper." Dad rubbed his bloodshot eyes. "I've been crunching numbers since noon. I need to get out. You heard of this Piggly's restaurant?"

Brian nodded. "Big" Aaron Pineeda talked about it all the time, since his dad owned the place.

Dad put his arm around Brian's shoulders and pulled him along. "All right, then. Let's go."

A little cyclone of dust spun in the wind as Dad pulled the car into the gravel lot at Piggly's. The building had been painted a bright shade of pink, and the sign by the road, lit by pink neon lights, read *Piggly's: Home of the Legendary Big Porker Sandwich.* An enormous pink pig balloon sat up on the roof, twenty-five feet across with a smile six feet wide. It looked like it was dancing as it jiggled in the breeze. Dad parked and they got out.

Brian opened the front door of the restaurant, and immediately an *oink-oink, oink-oink* sounded from a speaker on the wall. A bald man with a big belly spun away from the front counter where he had been talking to a bored-looking high school girl. He flashed a huge grin and held out his arms, looking a little like the grinning pig on the front of his apron. "Welcome! Welcome! Welcome to Piggly's, gentlemen! I'm Ed Pineeda. Who might you be?"

Dad held out his hand. "Hi, I'm Jack Roberts."

Mr. Pineeda shook Dad's hand so hard that Dad's whole

body jiggled. "Nice to meet you, Jack! How can I please your palate tonight? Some slow-roasted succulent ribs with Piggly's SSSBS?"

Dad gave Brian a look like *Is this guy for real?* Brian had to ask. "What's that?"

"Piggly's Super Secret Special Barbecue Sauce!" Mr. Pineeda pinched together his thumb and forefinger, held them to his lips, and kissed them. "It's so sweet, so tangy. Just a little kick. Mmmm. You'll think you're in hog heaven — wait! You *are* in hog heaven! Ha! It'll make your mouth sing for joy! I'll maybe start you with one of my noodle salads what comes with olives shipped in on a special armored truck from a secret supplier out of Des Moines!"

"It all sounds great," said Dad. "Maybe we could just see a menu?"

"Certainly! Come right this way. I'll get you a table and a couple menus. Lists of all the heavenly dee-lights that you'll find here at Piggly's." Mr. Pineeda led them to a table and clapped his hands. "I'll leave you gentlemen to the agony of choosing just a few treats from our broad selection, and the lovely Miss Kendra Hanson will be over in a bit to take care of you."

They looked over the menus. Eventually, the high school girl came over, wearing a pink plastic pig snout on her nose. Dad put his fist over his mouth, trying to hide his laughter, but if this made the girl mad, she didn't show it. "Hi welcome to Piggly's home of the Big Porker I'm Kendra I'll be your waitress tonight may I take your order?" she said all in one breath, without really looking at either of them. Brian sometimes felt bored when going over fractions in math class, but he'd never been as bored as this girl had just sounded.

They ordered a couple of sodas and their food, then a silence fell over the table. Brian and his father used to talk all the time. Tonight, though, neither seemed to have much to say. He looked around the restaurant. A number of plaques hung on the walls for things like *Riverside's Best Restaurant* and *Best Barbecue* with the years of the awards. There were a few red and white Riverside Roughriders pennants. A shelf on another wall held bowling trophies and some pictures of Little League baseball teams wearing Piggly's-sponsored uniforms.

A big pink pig on a poster on the wall behind Dad shouted in huge letters, *PIGGLY'S PIG-OUT CONTEST*. Brian read the details. The first contestant to eat a one-pound barbecue pork sandwich — the Big Porker — plus a side of Pig Tails, otherwise known as curly fries, would win Mr. Piggly, the huge, grinning pink balloon up on the roof. A whole pound of barbecue pork? That sounded awesome.

Dad's voice pulled him out of his thoughts. "You know, I don't really know anything about what you've been up to lately," he said. Kendra brought the sodas over and thumped them down on the table. Dad switched his Pepsi with Brian's

Mountain Dew, which had been placed in front of him. He ran his fingers back through his hair. "I'm sorry I've been so . . . well . . . distant lately. It's just . . . work, you know."

Brian did know. Lately, when Dad talked, that was all he talked about.

"And I've been tense and no fun. I'm sorry. It's just that we're having trouble finding the money we need to make more Plastisteel and to make it faster. I thought Mrs. Douglas was going to come through, but she won't accept just a simple demonstration. No, she's like a kid playing with her money, and she wants us to build her some toys. She wants us to make her a Plastisteel car or robot or airplane or . . ."

Brian looked up sharply. "Don't worry, Dad," he said. "Things will work out."

"We're running out of time. There's just no way we can synthesize enough Plastisteel for an effective demonstration that fast! If we don't get a cash infusion soon . . ." Dad noticed Brian staring at him. "Sorry, buddy. You don't want to hear about any of this stuff. Remember how I talked about taking a risk in order to achieve something great? Well, the thing about risk is that it can bring great success." He took a drink of soda, but coughed. "Or it can bring failure."

Brian couldn't remember seeing his father like this before. He looked terrible, all shabby and worn down. There were dark circles under his eyes, and was that gray hair above his ears? If Dad needed money so badly, maybe Brian could convince Alex and Max to just hand the flyer over to

Synthtech now so Dad and Dr. Warrender would have something to show Mrs. Douglas. He wanted to tell Dad about it, but he'd made a promise to the guys. He couldn't betray them by ruining the whole secret.

"You're not going to fail, Dad," Brian said. "I really think your Plastisteel will impress that lady." The flyer would make sure of that.

"I never give up, Brian," Dad said quietly. "We're exploring all options, but I think you should prepare for some tough times. I'm . . . I'm sorry I brought you to Iowa. I took you away from everything in Seattle. . . ."

"No, Dad. It's really great here. I'm having fun," Brian said. It wasn't a total lie. "I've been hanging out with Alex and Max. I can skateboard right in the street. And there's the cool skate park." Plus Wendy, as long as Frankie wasn't around.

"Really?"

"Oh yeah," Brian said. "And here there's a waitress who has to wear a pig snout."

Dad laughed. Brian had never heard a better sound. "Well, thanks for that. Knowing you're getting along okay here makes me feel a lot better. Listen, don't worry about my business problems, all right? You just focus on school and making friends. All that normal stuff sixth grade boys are supposed to do. Okay?"

Brian nodded as the waitress brought their food. Sure, he should focus on the normal stuff — like secret workshops and homemade airplanes. But he couldn't ignore Dad's problems with the Plastisteel business, and it was time to do something about it.

That night after supper, Brian called Alex and Max for an emergency meeting in the Eagle's Nest.

"No way!" Alex said as soon as Brian suggested they give up the flyer. "This is really what you called us here for? We've worked too hard on this thing. If the grown-ups get the plane, we'll never get to fly it, and then we've lost all those publicity opportunities and the chance for big money." He looked around as if worried someone else besides Brian and Max might be listening. When he spoke again, he was quieter. "Plus, our car dealership — it isn't doing too good. My dad acts like everything's fine, but our credit won't hold out forever."

"So maybe you won't get the newest iPhone," said Brian. "For me, this is a bigger deal." Alex opened his mouth as if to say something, but Brian cut him off. "If Synthtech goes bankrupt, I'll probably have to move again, and you can bet nobody will be using my grandpa's shed like this if that happens."

"I agree with Alex," Max said. "We cannot give up the flyer. It isn't ready to fly. It would be humiliating to present my mother and father with a project that does not work. They already have enough doubts about the likelihood of my future success."

Brian paced to the far end of the workshop. "We have to do something!"

"But not give up the flyer," said Max.

"Exactly," said Alex. "There has to be another way to make this rich lady get the picture about how cool Plastisteel is without ruining our plans."

Brian spun to face Alex. "What did you say?"

"Dude, we're keeping the —"

"No, you said 'get the picture'!" Brian hit himself in the forehead. "I'm an idiot!"

"What?" Max asked.

"It's so easy," said Brian.

"What?" Alex asked.

"Your phone can take photos and videos, right?" Brian said to Alex.

Alex took his iPhone out. "This baby can do anything."

"I'll call Mrs. Douglas and arrange a meeting," said Brian. "She keeps saying she wants to see a Plastisteel car or even a plane. We'll take her photos and a video of the flyer as proof that Plastisteel can be awesome. If we do a good job with our presentation, we'll impress her enough to invest in the company."

Max tilted his head. "This is likely the best we can do under the circumstances."

Alex began circling the flyer. "You make the appointment. I'll get photos and a video."

"Mrs. Douglas lives in Iowa City," said Max. "How will we get there?"

"Leave that to me," Alex said. "Good idea, Brian."

The next evening after school, Brian, Max, and Alex found themselves crammed into the backseat of Matt Karn's aging Oldsmobile Alero, along with all of Matt's sweaty football gear. The car smelled like a mix of greasy fries, chopped onions, and rotten tomatoes.

"So, Alex, is it true that my brother owes you five bucks after the Dysart game?" Matt spoke loudly, watching Alex, Brian, and Max in the rearview mirror. Matt was David's older brother, and the only teenager Alex could bribe to drive them to Iowa City. There was some kind of Thursday night football team supper at a pizza buffet, and Alex had offered Matt ten dollars to drop the three of them off at the mall on his way.

"Sorry, dude," Alex said. "I have to bet on the winner. It's just business."

Matt frowned. "Yeah? Who'd you pick to win this week?"

"Are you kidding me?" Alex was in his smooth business mode. "You and the Roughriders will crush Lone Tree."

"Yeah we will! Playoffs this year, baby!" Matt punched the steering wheel as he pulled his car up to the curb in front of the mall. His eyes found Alex in the mirror and his smile vanished. "Now give me ten bucks. How's that for business?"

Alex handed over the money.

"Great. Get out of my car. Meet me here at eight. If you're late, you can walk the twelve miles back to Riverside."

Brian took a deep breath of clean air when he got out of the car. "That guy seriously needs to do some laundry."

Alex scanned the parking lot as he spoke. "David said that Matt thinks he'll run the luck out of his clothes if he washes them."

Max wiped his glasses off on his shirt. "I believe he is risking infection by any number of strains of bacteria that must be breeding in his sweat-soaked —"

"There's our cab!" Alex said.

The three of them climbed into the back of the taxi that Alex had arranged to pick them up, and Alex gave the driver the address. They couldn't afford a taxi all the way from Riverside to Mrs. Douglas's house in Iowa City, and they couldn't let Matt Karn know where they were really going. Now that they were on their way to the meeting, Brian's stomach felt inside out, the way it did when Dad used to throw the Cardinal into quick little dives.

"Okay, gentlemen," said Alex. "Time to look classy. Ties."

Brian pulled his necktie out of his bag. Matt had already made fun of them for their khaki pants and shirts with buttons. The ties would have completely signaled that something funny was up. All three of them slipped their ties on and tightened them. Brian leaned forward in the seat and faced Alex. "Does this look right?"

Alex checked Brian and Max over. "Very professional. Just remember to take these things off before we catch our ride with Matt back at the mall."

Brian nodded. How could he forget to take this stupid thing off? The tie was so tight on his neck that he felt he was on his way to his own execution.

When they arrived at Mrs. Douglas's address, Alex paid the driver and the three of them climbed out of the car. The after-sunset glow was dimming in the west, but the night wasn't any darker in front of this house. On either side of a big round-top wooden front door were large lights that looked like old oil lanterns from castle movies. The house itself was built out of tan stone blocks and looked like a fortress for a king or queen.

"This house must be worth at least a million dollars," Max said.

"I like this lady already," said Alex.

Brian led the way up to the house. Small black lamps lined both sides of the cement path. They paused on the front porch. To the right of the door was the glowing orange button for the doorbell. All they had to do was press it.

"Are you guys ready for this?" Brian asked.

"Dude, this will be easy," Alex said. "Let me do the talking."

Brian tried to will his legs to stop shaking, but couldn't. After all, Mrs. Douglas had intimidated even Dad, who always had, or used to have, an answer for everything. He swallowed. *Great success through great risk.* He pressed the button to ring the doorbell and a series of chimes rang inside, like classical music.

Something clicked, and the door swung open to reveal Mrs. Douglas in black pants and a sweater with a flower pattern. She smiled when she saw them. "Well, aren't you boys just the picture of charming little professionals. Please come in."

Brian let Alex lead the way into a room with antique furniture, a large fireplace, and a grand piano. The heavy door thudded shut behind them.

"The office is this way, boys." Mrs. Douglas's shoes tapped the hardwood floor all the way down the hallway. She led them into a room lined with bookshelves crowded with old and expensive-looking leather-covered books. Her shiny wooden desk was in the center of the room. Four high-backed leather chairs, the kind with the little round brass buttons along the fronts of the armrests, waited in front of it. She sat down behind her desk. "Please," she said, motioning for them to sit.

Brian, Max, and Alex sat. Mrs. Douglas seemed to study each of them. The room was absolutely silent for what seemed like a very long time. Finally, she took a breath and sighed. "Boys, I'm a very busy woman. If I wanted to sit here with someone quiet, I'd call my husband in." She tapped her lower lip.

Alex stood up. "Good evening, ma'am, I'm Alex.

Thank you for letting us come see you tonight. I'd like to begin by —"

"What's your last name, Alex?" Mrs. Douglas said.

"Mackenzie, ma'am. I'm Alex Mackenzie. This is Brian Roberts and Max Warrender." He nodded to each of them.

Her eyes narrowed. "Are you any relation to the Mackenzie Lexus dealer here in town?"

"That's my father's dealership, ma'am."

Brian watched Alex. He looked completely comfortable. How did he do it? Where had he learned all this "ma'am" stuff? He sounded like he'd been in the army.

"Hmm," she said. "I wouldn't even waste my time with you boys, but Brian here tells me there's been a major breakthrough with Plastisteel. *Except* . . . I'm not supposed to discuss this with Mr. Roberts or Dr. Warrender. A secret? I'm mildly interested." She pulled back her sleeve and checked her gold watch. Brian thought he caught a glimpse of diamonds on it. "You have exactly five minutes."

"Thank you, Mrs. Douglas," Alex said. He activated a smile. "Should you choose to wisely invest in this incredible new invention of my friend's mother —"

"Don't even try to give me advice about my investments, boy. I'll decide what's wise and what's not. Now get to the point."

Alex's smile vanished. "I'm sorry. I didn't mean . . . well . . . I just wanted . . ."

Mrs. Douglas sighed loudly. "Four minutes left!"

Max cleared his throat. "Mrs. Douglas, you have informed my mother and Brian's father that you'd like to see a more impressive demonstration of the potential of Plastisteel. You particularly suggested that you might like to see some sort of Plastisteel vehicle."

"I'm not in the business of suggesting. I have so much money coming in that I can barely keep track of it all. If I can make a few bucks on this magic plastic stuff, then fine, but I gotta have fun doing it!"

"Precisely." Max motioned for Brian to show her the photos. "In order to accommodate your desire for proof of Plastisteel's potential, we thought we should show you these photographs of a Plastisteel airplane we have constructed."

Brian held the photographs out to Mrs. Douglas, and she snatched them from his hands. She flipped through a few images before spreading them out on the desk in front of her. "Hmm," she said. "You boys built this thing?"

"Yes, ma'am," Brian said.

She opened the center drawer of her desk and pulled out a magnifying glass to examine the pictures. After a moment she looked up at them. "Where did you get all this magic plastic?"

"Well, my mother. She . . . let me use some of her prototype materials," Max said.

An amused expression crept across Mrs. Douglas's face. "Oh, she did, did she?" She folded her hands on top of her desk. "Now, why do I find that so hard to believe?

Does your mama know that you boys have made this airplane?"

"Actually, ma'am," Max said, "we were rather hoping that we could count on your continued discretion. It would probably be better if our parents didn't know about this project at the moment."

She let out something like a laugh. "That's what I thought."

Alex took his phone from his pocket. "Mrs. Douglas, I could show you video of the flyer if you want."

"Does it show this airplane of yours flying?" Mrs. Douglas asked.

"Um . . . no, ma'am."

"Now why should I be interested in a bunch of pictures and a little home movie of an aircraft that's not airborne?"

"I'm sure you can understand that the business of Plastisteel aircraft could be very lucrative, especially —"

She pointed at Alex. "You're done talking."

Alex nodded and sat down.

Max said, "Mrs. Douglas, I've made some charts and graphs to explain my theories on the potential of —"

"If I don't want one child's business advice, I certainly don't want another kid's boring science junk." Mrs. Douglas checked her watch. "One minute left, boys."

Brian didn't even think. There was no time, and they simply could not afford to fail. He stood up out of his seat and approached the desk. "Why do you want to wait for something Dr. Warrender and my dad can make sometime in the future, when you can see this awesome airplane right now?" He pointed at the photos in her hands. "Just look at her. Imagine what it would feel like to soar through the air in this. With Plastisteel, she's lighter than any other plane out there, and she's, well, nearly unbreakable. Working on this flyer and being at her controls has been . . . just . . . awesome. Plastisteel is as great as our parents say it is." Brian took a breath. "That's why I hope you'll tell my dad that you'll invest with Synthtech."

Mrs. Douglas looked up from her watch. "And with ten seconds to spare," she said. She locked her eyes on Brian's. "Have you flown this plane?"

"For a very short flight," Brian said. "We're still working to —"

"Do you think it's going to fly?"

"Absolutely," he said. "I know she will."

She raised her eyebrows. "I almost like you, boy. You seem to have guts. But I am tired of vague promises. If you can show me proof of this plane of yours flying, I'll invest my money in your daddy's company. *And* I'll forget to tell them about you boys and all that magic plastic that you somehow got your greedy hands on."

"Thank you, Mrs. Douglas," Brian said. He swallowed.

She stood up. "Don't thank me. Show me the proof.

Don't you dare bother me again unless you have that shiny little airplane of yours up and flying. You understand?"

"Yes, ma'am," they all said together.

"Well, ain't that sweet?" she said. "Now get out of my office and run along home. I expect you boys have work to do."

"Jack, you've been at it all week." Mom said to Dad in the kitchen. "I think you can take a little break. Church is only an hour."

"Believe me, Diane, I can't."

Brian sat down at the dining-room table. They were doing that whole talking-quiet-so-nobody-would-think-anything-was-wrong thing. Usually, he would ditch out to his room whenever Mom and Dad were arguing, but this time he hung around, hoping Dad would win. No way did he want to go to Mom's old church. All those old people that Grandpa knew, all telling Brian how much he'd grown and that he probably didn't remember them . . . No kidding he wouldn't remember them! He had been five or something the last time he had gone to church in Iowa.

"Mary needs help installing the new security system before the next batch of Plastisteel is ready this week."

"So it's 'Mary' now, is it?"

"What is that supposed to mean?"

"You see more of that woman than you do your own family!"

"What?" Dad said. They both got a lot quieter. For a little while, Brian could only hear rumbles of angry talk.

"An hour, Jack. Just church as a family. We haven't even been to one service since we moved here. I think it would be good for us and for Brian. You promised you'd take time for your family."

"You don't understand. We're finally just starting to replace our stock of Plastisteel," Dad said. "If there's another theft, we are bankrupt!"

Another theft? What was he talking about? Brian stood up and went to the kitchen door. Mom said something, but he couldn't make out her words.

"No! It can't wait!" Dad shouted.

"Keep your voice down!" Mom said.

"I already waited too long," Dad said. "If we would have had better security back before Mary moved her lab to Iowa City, we might not have been ripped off."

It was quiet after that. Brian was about to put his ear to the door when he heard footsteps approaching. He rushed for a chair at the table and pulled the newspaper close to him.

Dad came out of the kitchen and stopped suddenly. "Hey, buddy. I didn't realize you were sitting right there." Brian kept his eyes fixed on the newspaper, though he had no idea what the article was supposed to be about. Dad glanced at the paper. "Reading the farm report, I see."

Brian knew he should say something to smooth out the situation — something funny or cool like Alex would say. But he just sat frozen in his chair.

"I don't know how much you heard," Dad said. "Just . . . don't worry, okay? Everything will be fine. You'll see."

"Yeah," he said. "It's cool."

"I could just really use this time," said Dad. "I'll make it up to you and Mom. I promise." He mussed Brian's hair as he headed off through the living room toward his office.

Brian used to hate it when Dad messed with his hair. He didn't mind as much anymore.

Mom leaned against the door frame. She was already wearing her nice clothes. "Go up and get dressed," she said. "I put your church clothes out for you."

As Brian took his seat in a hard wooden pew at church, Grandpa shuffled in next to them. "Morning, Diane. Brian. Where's Jack?"

Brian could feel Mom stiffen next to him. She pulled a hymnal from the slot on the back of the pew in front of them. "He had to work."

"Ah." Grandpa coughed a little and cleared his throat. "I see. Well, there'll be other services."

Wendy took a seat a few rows ahead of them, smiling and waving when she saw Brian. He couldn't make himself return as happy a greeting, and Wendy's expression faded a bit as she faced the front. Even though he was feeling down, he should have tried to look happier to see her. He loved the way she looked in her blue dress.

He tried to pay attention to the hymns and prayers, but there was one thing he couldn't get out of his mind. Some Plastisteel had been stolen. That was why Dad complained about not having enough for the demonstration with Mrs. Douglas. Someone had robbed him of his best chance to get the company out of money trouble.

He thought of the look on Mrs. Douglas's face and the sneer in her voice while she asked Max where he got the Plastisteel for the flyer. Max had stammered worse than Brian had when Ms. Gilbert grilled him on the first day of school. Dad had said the lab had been moved to Iowa City after the theft. It must have been here in Riverside before that. And if Dr. Warrender worked on the Plastisteel at home . . .

It all added up to one conclusion. Max was a thief. He had stolen the Plastisteel from his own mother and then lied about it. Now Synthtech was on the edge of failure, and Brian's parents were fighting because of it.

The pastor was delivering the sermon. Something about forgiveness and peace. Those were the last things on Brian's mind.

After church, Brian changed quickly into jeans and a T-shirt. Without even bothering to ask his parents if he could go out, he grabbed *Spitfire* and tore off up the street toward the Eagle's Nest. He hoped Max was there, for Max's sake, because otherwise Brian was going straight to Max's house. And Max probably wouldn't want Brian on his case about the Plastisteel in front of his mother.

Leaving his skateboard outside, he went into the Eagle's Nest, coming up out of the tunnel to see Max and Alex laughing at a Weird Al video on Alex's phone. It was *great* to see them acting like such pals, Brian thought savagely. Great that Alex seemed to be getting over his problem about hanging out with Max. Really terrific.

"Dude!" Alex said when he spotted Brian. "You're just in time. We've been working all morning and we finished the wing. Now Max is putting the last touches on the engine."

Brian reached over and paused the video on the phone.

"Hey, we were watching that," Alex said. "Max kept asking me to play it. Finally, I gave in. It's really funny stuff."

Max watched Brian with an even expression. "Unless I am very mistaken, something is troubling you."

Brian put his hands on the table and leaned toward Max. "How did you really get the Plastisteel to build the flyer?"

Max turned away for a moment, almost as if he were about to ask the cardboard Captain Kirk for advice. "I told you. My mother . . . she had extra and she —"

"Liar!"

Alex put his hands up. "Whoa! Chill. No need to freak out and start —"

"You stole it!" Brian moved around to Max's side of the table. Max staggered back. "I know all about it. My dad said they had all this Plastisteel when the lab was still in Riverside and it was stolen. If it takes them so long to make the stuff, your mom wouldn't have just given you this much to play with!"

Max had circled around the other corner of the table and squeezed past Alex. Brian followed him. "I was so stupid! An *idiot* to think that your mom just said, 'Here, son, I have some extra industrial-strength sheets of super plastic and I want *you* to have them. Just for fun!' You stole from our parents' company and lied to everyone!"

Alex looked at Max. "Is this true?"

"Well." Max took his glasses off and rubbed his eyes. "Sort of. I mean. Mostly. Just let me —"

"My mom and dad invested everything they had in this company! I had to move all the way to stupid Iowa! Where this stupid guy will be born!" Brian punched cardboard Kirk in the chest, knocking him back to the wall.

"Don't take it out on Captain Kirk!" Max said.

Brian spun to face him. "No, I'm going to take it out on you."

He lunged toward Max, but Alex moved between them. "Just calm down a second, Brian. We gotta work this out." Brian shoved him out of the way. "Dude, chill! You about made me drop my phone!"

"Oh, I'm so sorry for nearly wrecking your phone! Your rich father would have had to buy you a brand-new one."

"You think your family is the only one going through tough times?" Alex yelled, shaking his iPhone in the air. "I didn't even want this thing in the first place, but my dad thinks it's important to have all the best stuff. Reputation, success, blah blah blah. If this breaks now, my dad will kill me, and he can't buy me a new one."

"Guys, stop fighting! I'm sorry!" Max shouted louder than Brian had ever heard him. His glasses were off and he wiped his eyes. Nobody spoke or moved. "I'm sorry for lying. I should have been honest with you. I didn't realize that Plastisteel was so difficult to synthesize back when I acquired . . . *stole* it," he said. "I thought this was a relatively small quantity that wouldn't be missed, given the massive volume they would eventually manufacture. By the time I realized how much trouble my theft had caused, they had already filed police reports. My mother was so angry about it that I lacked the courage to confess what I had done."

Something twisted inside Brian. Here he was screaming at Max for lying. But how many times had Brian lied to avoid going to lunch with Max? Which was worse, being a hypocrite like Brian or a thief like Max?

"Well, you'll have to confess now," he said. "You'll give the Plastisteel back. They might not punish you that much since your mom —"

"Wait a minute," Alex said. "It isn't that simple. We've been working on the flyer for like a month now. We all showed it off to Mrs. Douglas together. You can't just go to the cops and tell them that you've had this stolen property for so long. We'll get . . . I don't know . . . second-degree theft, or conspiracy to steal Plastisteel —"

"That's not a real criminal charge," said Max.

"Well, something!" Alex said. "Like it or not, Brian, we're all in this now. Together."

"Yeah, well, that's great," Brian said. "So my family will be bankrupt now because of this, *and* the three of us are going to jail." Oddly enough, being involved in something with Alex was a big part of why Brian had agreed to work on the flyer. Too bad neither of them had realized they were getting themselves wrapped up in a crime.

"What happened to getting the flyer in the air, impressing that rich lady?" Alex said.

Brian examined the mostly reassembled engine. "Is she ready to fly?" he asked Max quietly.

Max kept his eyes fixed on the floor. "With the drag from the skateboard wheels, I don't think we have quite enough power to reach a true takeoff speed." He slipped his glasses back on. "I have some solid theories for improving engine power, but to implement them, I'll need . . . more Plastisteel."

Brian said nothing. Max was a good guy in the end, but now it seemed they were all stuck in a hopeless situation. He didn't know what to do, but he knew he needed to get away from all of this, at least for a little while. He went out, grabbed *Spitfire*, and left.

The next morning, Brian left the house early and rolled down to the ramps at Riverview Park. He was tired of thinking about the whole stolen Plastisteel thing. It was good just to move, to skate out his trouble. He popped up over one of the smaller ramps, sailing through a good two feet of air before his wheels hit the cement. He wobbled a little. Sloppy landing.

He kicked *Spitfire* faster, then stomped her tail to jump her up, grinding her trucks along the edge of a steel rail. He didn't kick off right on the dismount, though, and had to jump clear and come to a running stop. Stupid. That was an easy trick. Skating was the last thing in his life that wasn't messed up, and he was messing up every trick he tried that morning.

"I was hoping I'd find you here."

Wendy stood at the edge of the skate park, her skateboard leaning against her leg. She put down her backpack and took off her white jacket. She had on a sleeveless flower-print shirt with wide straps over the shoulders and lace at the bottom. Brian hooked his upside-down board with his toe and flipped it back onto its wheels. He usually found clothes boring, but somehow he always seemed to notice what Wendy wore.

He hopped on *Spitfire* and rolled around in a tight circle. Wendy dropped her skateboard to the cement and rolled in an opposite arc. They skated around and around, facing each other.

"How did you know I was down here?"

"The other day you skated past my street on the way to school," Wendy said with a grin. "You couldn't have been coming from your house. I asked myself where you might have been, then I took a guess and rolled down here to find out if I was right."

"Yeah, but why?" Brian kicked his skateboard out of the circle they'd been running, guiding *Spitfire* in a gentle curve toward the stairs to the half-pipe.

Wendy skated after him. "Because one thing Frankie will absolutely not do is wake up really early to follow me." She joined him up on the half-pipe deck. "And you looked kind of down in church yesterday."

On any other day Brian would have felt almost dizzy if a beautiful girl like Wendy had come all the way to the skate park to find him. "Sorry," he said. "A lot on my mind."

"Anything I can help you with?"

"Not unless you can help me fly."

She elbowed him lightly. "I thought you were best at that."

Brian put his back truck over the lip at the edge of the ramp and looked down into the half-pipe. "I keep trying to get a high enough jump make a complete 360. I can never quite get enough air." He stomped the front of his board down hard and dove into the drop. Transition. Flat. Transition. Up! He cleared the other side and cranked *Spitfire* around in the air. He put the wheels back on the ramp and rolled back toward Wendy. In the air again, he tried to twist around for the 360 but wasn't fast enough.

His wheels hit the ramp and he felt the board slow down just a little from the drag. He bent his legs to shoot up the other side and soared into in the air, twisting *Spitfire* in a half spin. Nothing slowed him up here — no gravity, no drag, just flying.

That was it!

He landed backward, skating for a while, but then waxing out in the flat bottom.

"Are you okay?" Wendy called down to him. "You almost had it!"

Brian's knees and elbow hurt, but he stood up with a smile. "I've got it! Everything is going to be great!"

The flyer couldn't get into the air because the engine didn't have enough power to overcome the drag and reach takeoff speed. But what if it wasn't slowed down by rolling along on the runway? What if there was a way to get rid of that drag force?

They both skated around the park for a while longer before heading off to school. A plan was coming together in Brian's mind. It was totally crazy. The odds were still stacked against them. But it just might work.

Brian spent most of that day waiting for his chance to get back to the Eagle's Nest. He only had to put up with a couple body checks from Frankie — more minutes off his time spent with Wendy. At least the idiot hadn't figured out that he skated with her that morning. When the class was dismissed for lunch, Brian stayed at his desk as he did most days, sketching out his plan, until Ms. Gilbert kicked him out of the room. When he finally made his way to the cafeteria, he didn't even bother with the lunch line, but simply took his pencil and notebook to an empty table and kept working.

That afternoon Brian was the first one out of the school. He stopped on the way to the Eagle's Nest to buy a bag of cheese puffs and three Mountain Dews. Hopefully the soda would help smooth things over a little after his outburst yesterday — that, and the new plan.

At the Eagle's Nest, Brian admired the flyer. Her streamlined wings and tail. The engine that was now mostly back together. She looked good, and she was going to fly. Soon.

Max came up out of the tunnel. "Brian, I didn't expect you to be here." He wouldn't meet Brian's eyes.

"Alex coming?"

Max nodded. "I talked to him on the street out front. He's going to get his iPod speakers, and then he'll be right over."

Brian put his bag on the east wall workbench, taking out his notebook. He saw the dent he'd made in cardboard Captain Kirk's chest.

"I'm very sorry for not telling you sooner about the stolen Plastisteel," Max said. "I should never have stolen it in the first place. I just thought my parents might be impressed if I could show them a working flyer."

Alex came up into the workshop. "Oh," he said when he saw Brian. "What did I miss?"

"Max," said Brian, "you shouldn't have stolen the Plastisteel, but Alex was right yesterday. We're all in this together now. We have to get this flyer airborne so we can impress Mrs. Douglas and get her to, well, basically save Synthtech."

Brian was about to go on, but Max held up his hand to speak. "I might have improved the engine capacity by a very small amount, but there's only so much I can do without more Plastisteel. I don't believe the engine has enough power to overcome the drag."

That was exactly what Brian had hoped he would say.

"Bingo," he said. "What if I told you there's a way to eliminate all ground drag on takeoff?"

"That's impossible, right?" Alex said. "I mean, they're skateboards, not hoverboards. You're going to have some resistance from the wheels on the runway."

"We're not going to take off from a runway." He rolled out his drawing. It showed the flyer hanging by three cables from a giant balloon. A close-up sketch in the corner detailed the steel ring-and-pin release system that would attach the cables to the flyer.

"You propose to lift the flyer into the air?" Max said.

"Yeah," said Brian. "We fill our balloon with helium and hoist the flyer really, really high. Then we start the engine in the air. The flyer won't have any problem building up speed since it'll already be off the ground."

"We'll never be fast enough," Alex said. "The balloon will be a giant parachute."

"Once we top out our speed and we're dragging the balloon, we release the cables."

"But your lack of forward velocity would then put the flyer into a rapid descent," Max said.

"Big deal," Brian said. "We'd be high up, and we'd be level. I just dip the nose forward a little and then level off. She'd come out of the fall and be flying under her own power with hundreds of feet to spare."

Alex looked from Max to Brian and back again. "You seriously think this could work? Where do we even get a giant balloon?"

"This Saturday night, Mr. Pineeda is having a Pig-Out Contest where the prize is Mr. Piggly himself," said Brian. "All you have to do is finish a Big Porker sandwich and some Pig Tails. I may not look like a big eater, but I can pack food away. I'm going to win that balloon." Brian had taken first place in a hot-dog eating contest back in Seattle, devouring eight disgusting school dogs in one lunch period. He was older now, and this was actually good food. He could win this.

"Finding that much helium may pose a problem." Max leaned over the diagram, looking from the picture to the flyer. "Otherwise, I think this is an excellent plan. It may interest you to know that the first space shuttle, named *Enterprise* after the ship from *Star Trek*, did not first take off under its own power. It was taken up on top of a 747 and launched in atmospheric flight tests from there."

"Wow, more lame *Star Trek* stuff," said Alex. He chugged down the rest of his soda and tapped Brian's drawing. "Dude, this is really cool, but if this is the plan, flying under a giant pig, we better finish putting the engine back together."

The week dragged on. Every day one of them read an article or watched a video online about eating contests. How much to eat. How much to drink. By Saturday, Brian felt as though he knew everything about how to eat a lot of food as quickly as possible.

That evening, Alex and Brian left Max in the Eagle's Nest and went down to Piggly's for the Pig-Out Contest. Brian breathed deeply, taking in the amazing smells of the place. He leaned toward Alex. "I'm ready to win."

Alex spoke quietly. "Win or lose, so many people are betting on this contest that I'm still going to make a ton of money."

"Good evening, boys!" Mr. Pineeda greeted them. "Young Mr. Mackenzie, and . . . Mr. Roberts, right?"

"Right," Brian answered.

"Ha! I knew it! I knew it! Just you two tonight? Coming for a taste of the truly extraordinary for dinner, or for the frozen dee-light, the treat that that can't be beat, Piggly's ice cream?"

Brian looked over to the tables in the dining area. A whole section of the room had been roped off, with a big pink sign advertising the Pig-Out Contest standing nearby. A couple of high school guys were already sitting at one of the tables, talking, laughing, and drinking sodas. Could he really out-eat high schoolers like that?

Alex elbowed him. Brian nodded and took his hands out of his pockets, his shoulders squared back. "I'm here to win the Pig-Out Contest," he said. "I want Mr. Piggly."

"That's the spirit!" Mr. Pineeda clapped his hands. "We need more big eaters like you in this town." He put his hand behind Brian's back and led him to the dining area. Alex followed. Mr. Pineeda unhooked the thick rope and motioned them through with his other hand. "Right this way, gentlemen. Take any seat you like. The contest begins in about twenty minutes. Miss Kendra Hanson will be around in a bit to take your drink orders."

Brian and Alex took the table farthest from the high school guys. One of them gave a nod, but the rest just ignored them.

"Remember what Max said about the stuff he looked up online," Alex said quietly. "Water only. No soda. The carbonation will only make you feel more full. You need to chew quickly, but really chew."

"I know," Brian said. "Chew the food up a lot so it's all compacted into a paste in my mouth before swallowing. That way it will take up less stomach space."

"A Big Porker is over a pound of food," Alex said. "The winner may be whoever can finish first, but the guys who stuff the food as fast as they can are going to feel too full to keep going."

Kendra the waitress approached the table. She put her hand on her hip and glanced back at the high school guys. "Want drinks?"

Alex's eyes traced her from her shoes all the way to the pig snout on her nose and the pink bow in her hair. He smiled at Kendra. "What happened to the nice greeting I've come to expect here at —"

"You want a soda or not?" She still didn't look at them. One of the high school guys had noticed her and made a snorting sound like a pig, then they all laughed and acted like they hadn't done anything. Her cheeks reddened.

"Don't pay attention to those guys," Alex said.

She glared at him. "Last chance. What do you want to drink?"

"Mountain Dew," said Alex. "Brian will just have water."

"Fine." She spun away so fast that her sandy brown hair flew back.

"And no Pig-Out Contest for me. I'll just have the Piglet Dinner."

She stopped and faced him. "Anything else?"

Alex shook his head. When she started toward the kitchen again, he elbowed Brian. "Check this out," he whispered. "Oh, and Kendra?" he said in a normal voice.

"What?" Kendra said impatiently.

"You have to be the only girl in the universe who can look pretty while being forced to wear that stupid pig nose."

She rolled her eyes. "Children," she said. But before she went away, Brian could see the hint of a smile on her face. Did Alex's line actually work? On a high school girl?

"Did you see that?" Alex said. "She totally likes me."

Maybe she did and maybe she didn't, but Brian never would have had the guts to do that. "Isn't she a little old for you?"

Alex shrugged. "She'll be a senior when we're freshmen. It could work. The secret to girls is confidence. That may be the secret to eating contests too."

Brian nodded. Why couldn't he have Alex's confidence? Why couldn't he always know the right thing to do? Instead, he always felt like he was making it up as he went along.

More people were coming in now. The tables in the contest section filled up mostly with kids, but there was also one guy who looked to be in his thirties. David and Red from their class sat down at their table, and so did Big Aaron Pineeda. "Dad said I could be in the contest, but if I win, the balloon will go to the second-place guy," said B.A. "He wants to get rid of it. It's getting old. A few weeks ago, one of the little metal rings that connects to the tie-down ropes actually broke. Mr. Piggly almost rolled right off the roof."

Brian thought it was good that B.A. couldn't win the balloon. Judging from his size, he would be tough to beat.

Jason Cooper showed up next. "I took money out of my car fund for this. If I win the pig balloon, I'm going to sell it on eBay. Probably enough to buy a whole set of tires, depending on what kind of car I get."

"Yeah, right, Cooper!" Frankie stepped over the rope into the contest area. "You'll be riding your sister's bike until you're twenty-five, because I'm going to win this contest tonight!"

Great, Brian thought. Just when he had a chance to hang out and have fun, here came the meanest tough guy in America to mess it all up.

Frankie caught sight of him. "Ah, the new boy is here. Good. I can beat him in something else."

Mr. Pineeda joined them. Kendra was right behind him, along with a man wearing a stained apron. They all carried big plastic trays filled with Big Porker Specials. "Okay, gentlemen, here's how the Pig-Out Contest works," Mr. Pineeda said. "Nobody can touch his plate until I say 'Go.' After that, the rules are simple. The first contestant to eat the entire one-pound dee-licious Big Porker sandwich" — Red raised his hand. Mr. Pineeda pointed at him — "bun included" — Red put his hand back down — "and finish all of his Pig Tails, will be the next proud owner of Mr. Piggly. He's twenty-five feet from snout to tail. Twenty feet across his midsection. Good for a parade or something, eh, boys?" Mr. Pineeda laughed.

Kendra and the cook began placing a plate in front of each contestant. She also put a plate with a much smaller sandwich in front of Alex. He might have said something flirty to her again, but Brian wasn't paying attention. He saw only the platter in front of him. The Big Porker looked as big around as a basketball and at least five inches high from bun to bun. Just the pile of shredded meat inside was probably as big as Alex's entire little Piglet. Could he even pick the sandwich up? How could he take a bite? The mountain of golden, steaming Pig Tails stood almost as high as the sandwich itself. How would he ever finish all of that?

"All right, boys. The plates are in position." Mr. Pineeda looked up and down the tables, checking for cheaters. "Nobody touch their food." Red held his hands inches above his sandwich. Frankie cracked his knuckles. Mr. Pineeda moved to the middle of the group of contest tables. He raised his hand up above his head. "Ready. Set. Go!"

He dropped his arm, and the contest was on. Brian tried to get his hands around the Big Porker and pick it up, but he kept getting SSSBS on them.

"Dude, there's no way you're going to be able to eat that thing and stay clean. Can't be done," Alex said. "Just go for it. Remember" — he lowered his voice to a whisper — "we *need* this."

Brian finally got ahold of the sandwich and took a big bite. He closed his eyes as he chewed. Mr. Pineeda was right. Piggly's served the best barbecue pork in the world. He added a bit of salt to the Pig Tails and crammed a curl in his mouth. After every bite he remembered Max's advice to chew a lot.

Across the table, Red's face was almost as red as his hair. He had barbecue sauce all over his mouth and cheeks. He'd taken off the bun and was forking huge clumps of meat into his mouth. "Itsh goo," he said, his mouth completely stuffed with pork.

"You still have to eat that bun," Alex said.

When Red could finally swallow, he spoke loudly with sauce still on his face. "I saw this video about a guy in Japan who wins hot-dog eating contests by dipping the bun in water. I figure Mountain Dew should do it too."

Brian kept eating, focusing on fries, while Red picked up the top bun, rolled and squished it into a sort of cigar shape, and then dipped it halfway down into his soda. Brian shook his head. Red slipped the soggy bun into his mouth and sort of slurped off the wet end, swallowing a second later.

"Easy," Red said. "Tastes pretty good too."

"You might have to try that trick," Alex whispered to Brian.

Brian tried not to gag at the thought. He took another big bite of his sandwich.

After about forty-five minutes, the guys were slowing down. David leaned forward, his face low to the table. Over half of his Big Porker was left. He looked at Red. "How did I let you talk me into this?"

"You're the one who said it would be easy. You love the barbecue pork here." Red frowned. "I don't know what's wrong with me tonight. I usually eat, like, two sandwiches like this for supper."

Alex laughed. "Red said!"

"Red said!" David moaned. He did not look up.

"Re shaid?" Brian mumbled while chewing. About half of his sandwich remained.

"It's something we say, usually at lunch, whenever Red . feeds us another one of his crazy stories," Alex said.

"It's true!" Red said. "Either two sandwiches like this, or a big buffalo steak."

Brian watched Frankie. He had maybe a quarter of his sandwich left and only a few Pig Tails. He let out a huge belch. "You sissies are going to have bad stomachaches for no reason when you see me walk out of here with the big prize." He caught Brian's gaze and flashed a sick grin, then held a Pig Tail up above his head, tilted his head back, and lowered the curly fry into his mouth.

No way. Not this time. Frankie was not going to beat him. Brian took the top bun off his sandwich, rolled it like Red had done, and dipped it in his water. Then he squished the soggy mass in his mouth. He didn't chew much. It sort of tasted pre-chewed anyway. He did the same thing with the bottom bun, then grabbed his fork and started shoving food in his mouth. Fries and pork together, it didn't matter. Food was food, and Brian had some catching up to do. ·

Alex had finished his tiny meal a long time ago, so he was going around the tables, confirming bets on his iPhone. Most of the high school guys seemed to have given up. They joked with one another, messed around on their phones, and took their time eating. The few guys who were still trying poked at their plates, maybe eating a fry once in a while. The old guy had left long ago. Brian stayed focused on his own plate. There were only four or five more forkfuls left.

He stabbed the last of his Pig Tails and brought the food to his mouth —

"Done!" Frankie shouted. He stood up, holding the empty plate above his head with both hands like a trophy. "I'm done. Who else is done? Nobody. I'm the winner!"

Seeing Frankie celebrate was enough to make Brian sick, and as full as he was, he didn't need much help.

"We have a winner!" Mr. Pineeda shouted. Everyone clapped, except for Brian, and David, who just moaned again.

Brian looked at the little bit of food he had left. He had taken a risk in this contest. A chance for greatness. A chance to fly. Now he had failed. Worse, he had let Dad down. They'd never get the flyer's engine fixed up enough to take off, not without extra parts. Mr. Piggly had been their only chance.

"You tried your best," Alex said quietly. "Maybe Frankie will just sell us the balloon. If not, we'll find another way to fly."

"There is no other way," Brian whispered.

"Well, what can we do about it?"

Frankie held his hand over his stomach as Mr. Pineeda told him how to handle Mr. Piggly.

That hand on the stomach. That was the giveaway.

"Hey, Frankie," Brian shouted. Frankie and Mr. Pineeda looked at him. "Bet you can't eat two!"

"What are you talking about?" Frankie snapped.

"Yeah, dude, what are you talking about?" Alex whispered.

"I bet you can't eat another Big Porker sandwich before I do," Brian said.

"Forget it. You lost. You're a loser." Frankie held his stomach and burped. "You're always a loser."

"Yeah? Hey, Frankie, maybe you'd rather order a *chicken* sandwich," Jason said.

Frankie glared at him. Mr. Pineeda laughed so hard he shook. "Uh-oh, Frankie. I think there's a challenge here . . . though *nobody* in the proud history of Piggly's has ever eaten two Big Porkers in one night."

"I can do it." Brian stood up. He was glad that he had the table there to steady him. He stared at Frankie. "Can you? If I win, I get the Mr. Piggly balloon. If you win, you get the balloon, plus I'll pay you ten bucks."

The high school guys started to chant, "Fran-kie! Fran-kie! Fran-kie!"

Brian could see the hatred in Frankie's eyes and knew he had him now. He sat back down and finished the food on his first plate.

"Fine!" Frankie held up his hands with his arms spread wide. "You guys want to see a new eating record. That's cool." He pointed at Brian. "Just the sandwich?"

"Just the sandwich," Brian said.

"This is amazing!" Mr. Pineeda said. "I'll be right back with two more Big Porkers!"

"Okay, okay!" Alex shouted. "It's Brian versus Frankie in the ultimate eating smackdown challenge." He held his iPhone above his head. "This contest is so hot, *I'm* going to take action on this. I got ten bucks on Brian right now! Any takers?"

Frankie slumped down in his seat. "Alex, my man! You gotta be kidding me! You don't think I can beat this guy?"

"Just business, Frankie," Alex said.

The other guys chimed in with their bets. The only one who didn't gamble on Frankie was David, who seemed to be in some sort of barbecue-pork coma and didn't bet at all.

The sandwiches were brought out. As soon as the new one was set down in front of Brian, everything else faded away. In all the world there was only Brian, his stomach, and the Big Porker.

He attacked the sandwich, forgetting all about the scientific methods he had studied. Slurping down another wet bun would have probably made him throw up anyway. Instead he forced down one bite while only partially chewing the next. Barbecue sauce glopped all over his mouth, cheeks, and fingers.

Finally, there was just one small blob of barbecue pork left. Brian wadded the meat up and held it in his hands, risking a look up at Frankie. Frankie was chewing furiously, trying to cram more and more into his mouth, but he had well over a quarter of his sandwich left. Brian had it. There was no way Frankie could win now.

He pushed the last of the food into his mouth and chewed the best he could, using his fingers to hold it all in until he could swallow. Slowly, he stood up. The light in the room seemed a bit blurred. "I win," he said. "Mr. Piggly is mine!"

Frankie slammed his fist down on the table.

Maybe some of the guys were clapping or whistling. With his painfully full stomach, Brian couldn't focus on them. Mr. Pineeda appeared next to him with a camera. "No, no," he said when Brian went for the napkins. "Leave the SSSBS on your face and wave with it on your fingers. Smile so everyone can see how happy you are after eating so much good food! I'll put this photo up on Piggly's Wall of Champions! You're our very first Double Big Porker Survivor!"

Alex collected a bunch of money. Someone, maybe Red, said something to Brian. Brian staggered out the door into the cool night air. The stars twinkled above in the night sky. "I won," he said to them.

Then he bent over and barfed until his throat felt raw.

11

On Monday morning, Ms. Gilbert stood in front of the class. "I am handing out the paper that describes your Greek mythology group assignment," she said. She quickly touched her thumb to her tongue so that she could separate the papers more easily, then peeled off enough for each row of students. Brian wished she wouldn't do the whole licking-the-thumb thing. It always left this gross glob of spit on the corner of the paper. It wasn't as bad for him in the fourth seat back, but he pitied the front-row people.

Starting in Wendy's corner, Ms. Gilbert counted off the students. "One, two, three. You're a group." She directed the next three into a group. Everyone looked around, trying to figure out who they'd be with. The first two people in Brian's row fell into a group with someone from the one before. That meant Alex, Brian, and Max would be working together.

"When I have given you permission to speak, and not a moment before then, you will form your groups," Ms. Gilbert said. Her shoes made that scary teacher *clip-clop* sound on the tile floor. "You will *not* drag your desks into position. You will lift them up off the floor and place them where you want them. Do you understand?"

Why did she always ask that? Brian wondered. Did she expect anyone to answer her? Whenever grown-ups asked, "Do you understand?" it seemed more like they were saying, "Do you understand how much trouble you'll be in if you don't do what I say?"

Ms. Gilbert continued. "Each group will choose one of the myths from the list on the paper. You will all read and study the story of the myth. Then you will do research online and in the library to find out how this myth appears in or affects our culture. You'll find advertisements, films, TV shows, novels, words, and . . ."

Something blinked on the screen of Brian's graphing calculator. It was an old model, one that his dad wasn't using anymore. He'd thought it was off. It blinked again and he looked more closely at it.

BRIAN, ARE YOU RECEIVING THIS
MESSAGE?
THIS IS MAX. PLEASE RESPOND AND
PRESS THE ZOOM BUTTON TO SEND.

Brian did his best to look like he was paying attention to Ms. Gilbert. He slid the calculator back behind his language arts book, hit the ALPHA LOCK key, and typed back:

HOW R U TXTING ME

He hit ZOOM. A moment later, another message appeared.

I APOLOGIZE FOR NOT TELLING
YOU ABOUT THIS EARLIER, BUT I
WASN'T SURE IF IT WOULD WORK. I
INSTALLED TRANSMITTERS INTO BOTH
OF OUR GRAPHING CALCULATORS,
SO WE NOW HAVE TEXT MESSAGE
CAPABILITY. HOWEVER, THE
TRANSMISSION RANGE ON THE
CALCULATORS IS LIMITED TO ABOUT
ONE HUNDRED FEET.

No wonder he hadn't been able to find his calculator over the weekend. It was cool that he could text in class, but really lame that it was on an old calculator. He wrote back:

WATS UP

Max's reply popped up quickly.

YOU MAY BE PLEASED TO KNOW
THAT PREFLIGHT CHECKS ON THE
REBUILT FLYER ARE COMPLETE, AND
THE STARBOARD WING IS FULLY
FUNCTIONAL. FURTHERMORE, ENGINE
REASSEMBLY IS FINISHED. I HAVE
PRODUCED A SUFFICIENT QUANTITY
OF HYDROGEN TO INFLATE MR. PIGGLY.
THE FORECAST TONIGHT CALLS FOR
CLEAR AND CALM. I BELIEVE WE
SHOULD ATTEMPT A FLIGHT THIS
EVENING.

Brian texted back.

YES FLY 2NITE Y NOT HELIUM

The answer came back:

IT'S GOOD THAT YOU ARE READY
TO FLY TONIGHT. I AM REASONABLY
CONFIDENT THAT THE FLIGHT WILL
BE A SUCCESS. AS REGARDS MY
CHOICE TO USE HYDROGEN RATHER
THAN HELIUM, BASICALLY IT IS A

MATTER OF HIT THE CLEAR BUTTON RIGHT NOW!

Brian tapped the CLEAR button, erasing the messages. He looked up just in time to see Ms. Gilbert a few paces away.

"What's so interesting back here, Brian?" she said. She picked up his calculator and frowned, then put it back down on his desk. "What myth do you suppose you'd like to work on with your group?"

Brian licked his lips. The secret seemed to be safe. "I think the Daedalus and Icarus story you told me about looks pretty cool."

"Have you read it yet?"

"I started it." He swallowed. "A long time ago."

"Ah, it's so *cool* that you haven't managed to finish reading it yet."

"Sorry. I'll read it now."

Ms. Gilbert tapped Brian's desk. "Stop fiddling with your calculator and pay attention." She *clip-clopped* back to the front of the room. Brian sat back in his desk and released a quiet sigh.

Later, as the class prepared to go to Mr. Carlson's room for science, Wendy put her hand on Brian's arm to stop him. "Hey, it's been a long time since we talked," she said.

He could have sworn her fingers were electrically charged. It tingled where she touched him, even after she took her hand away. "Yeah, um, I'm . . . sorry about that," Brian said.

Wendy leaned closer. "You want to skate tonight? We could carve it up on the half-pipe."

He wanted to more than anything, but he and the guys planned to fly that night. "I can't. Well, not tonight. I . . . um . . . I've got to help my grandpa on the farm. Otherwise, yeah, tonight would be awesome."

Wendy frowned a little. "Oh. You're busy a lot," she said. "That's too bad. Well, see you around." She headed out the door.

Brian saw Ms. Gilbert watching him from her desk. She raised an eyebrow. He hated lying to Wendy. Things would get better once they were flying. They had to.

That night, both Mom and Dad were home, so Dad made pork chops and potatoes. It was pretty tasty, and Brian would usually have eaten three or four chops and at least two scoops of potatoes, except that after the battle for Mr. Piggly last Saturday, Brian wasn't too crazy about pork just yet. More than that, by the time they sat down to eat, he was an hour late for the meeting at the Eagle's Nest.

"Brian, would you please relax and eat? It's still early. You can go play with your friends when you're done with supper."

Play? Why did adults call spending time with friends "playing"? He didn't have many friends, but he wouldn't make any more if anyone heard his mother treating him like a little kid. He tried to slow down and eat right so Mom wouldn't complain. Maybe he could divert their attention. "How's Synthtech, Dad?"

Dad offered a short smile. "Storm knocked the power out for a bit in Iowa City last night, but our security system kicked over to batteries and kept running." He chuckled. "I'd like to see anyone try to get their hands on the Plastisteel now."

Brian was grateful when the phone rang. Mom answered and then handed it to Brian.

"Hello?" Brian said.

"Dude, where are you?" Alex said. "We've been waiting for you."

"I'm almost done with supper. Then I'll be right over."

"Don't bother going to the Nest now. Max and I about killed ourselves, but we have everything set up at the place we used the first time. Hurry and get down here."

"I'll do my best," Brian said. He hung up the phone and went back to eating, speeding up a bit and hoping Mom wouldn't notice.

"Can I go now?" he asked when he'd finished.

"Is your homework done?" Mom said.

"Yes."

"What are you going to be doing?"

Brian sighed. "Skateboarding." It was sort of true. There were skateboards on the flyer.

Mom took a drink of water. "Just with Max and this Alex boy?"

"Oh, let him go already, Diane," Dad said. "Let him be with his friends. While he still can," he added quietly.

Mom closed her eyes for a moment, then waved Brian away from the table. Part of him felt bad for ditching them, but another part didn't want to stay around for the rest of a tense meal. He grabbed his backpack and headed out, dropping *Spitfire* to the pavement and kick-starting down the street. He was rolling close to the ground now, but soon he'd be flying.

"It's about time," Alex said when Brian reached the grain elevators. The enormous form of Mr. Piggly floated eight feet overhead, with two ropes staked in the ground holding it in place. Beneath the balloon, the flyer looked like it was ready for action.

"I said I was sorry," Brian said. "What's up?"

"Hopefully the flyer, in just a moment." Max said with a laugh. Alex shook his head. "Yes, well . . . Here's the plan." Max took his toy *Star Trek* phaser out of his pocket and pointed the red laser dot at a metal ring on the flyer's engine. "You see how the cable from Mr. Piggly attaches to the flyer at this ring. Brian, at the right moment, you must pull the pin, which will release the ring and cut the flyer loose from the balloon." Max used the phaser to point out two more rings on the skateboards below Alex's seat. "At the exact same moment, Alex, you must kick out both of these pins. Releasing all three metal rings at the same time is key to keeping the flyer balanced when you're breaking away from Mr. Piggly."

"So I start the engine when we're how high?" Brian asked.

"I'd say when you're over five thousand feet."

Brian frowned. "How do we know when we've over five thousand feet?"

"Chill, dude." Alex pulled a gadget about the size of his iPhone from his pocket. "I bought this altimeter online for about ten bucks. I figured we'd need it, since part of what we're doing tonight involves dropping from the bottom of the balloon."

"How do you order online?" Brian asked. "You have a credit card?"

Alex waved away the question. "Please. I know everything about money. I just buy Visa gift cards at the gas station." He shook the altimeter. "Anyway, this baby will tell us how high up we are."

"That's . . . actually incredibly helpful, Alex. Thank you," Max said.

Everything was set. Mr. Piggly smiled big above them. Brian put his hand to his stomach.

"How did you ever get enough hydrogen to fill this thing?" he asked. "And why not helium, anyway?"

"Ah, that's another issue." Max looked up at Mr. Piggly. "Helium is too expensive to buy in such large quantities. Hydrogen, on the other hand, floats even better, and can be produced through a process called electrolysis."

"Electrolysis?" Brian said.

"He rigged up this device to capture the gas," Alex said, "and then he ran an electric charge through water."

"Which separated the water's oxygen and hydrogen atoms," Max explained. "Hydrogen is flammable, but that won't be a problem. It's not as if we're exposing the balloon to any open flames."

Brian climbed into the pilot's seat. Alex sat down behind him. Brian went over the controls again, checking that it all worked.

"We've already checked the ailerons, rudder, and everything," Alex said. "Systems are all go."

Max stood at the front. "When the flyer is up to top speed, it should be pulling Mr. Piggly through the air like a ship dragging its anchor. That's when you separate. Remember, right after you're released, you should expect the flyer to fall a little bit. Keep her level and open the throttle. Once it gets up to speed, it should fly."

Brian took a deep breath. "Okay, Max. Release Mr. Piggly."

"Good luck, guys," Max said. He tugged on the stakes anchoring the balloon to the ground, but he couldn't get the ropes loose.

"Come on, Max!" Alex shouted. "You can do it! Be like Captain Kirk. He could pull those stakes up."

Max bit his lip and yanked hard again. The ropes fell away from Mr. Piggly and the flyer began to rise straight up into the air.

"Woo-hoo!" Alex yelled. "We have liftoff!"

"Yeah!" Max said. "Warp speed!"

The engine was off, so all was silent, but they were rising steadily. Everything on the ground seemed to shrink away beneath them. Max became smaller and smaller, then they cleared the treetops and kept going. To their left, they could see all of Riverside, the Catholic church steeple lit up brightly as always.

"Dude, this rocks!" Alex said.

Brian laughed. "We're really doing it! We're flying. Well . . . we're floating."

"You know what we need?" Alex said. "We need a name for this machine. We can't keep calling it 'the flyer.' You're supposed to give boats and bikes and planes and things cool girls' names, like Annabel or Suzie. Something like that. She needs a good name for good luck."

They reached the top of the grain elevators. Brian was sure that nobody had looked down on the tops of the giant cement cylinders in many years. They weren't quite as cool as the Space Needle back in Seattle, but still a good five or six stories high. The flyer floated above them now.

"What do you think?" Alex asked.

"It's awesome up here," Brian said.

"It is," said Alex. "But I mean about the name for the flyer."

"Oh. Well, you know how Ms. Gilbert was telling us about all the things named after Greek mythology? I was thinking about how the mission that took the astronauts to the moon was called *Apollo*. Maybe we could find a cool mythology name like that."

"Like Apollo? But that's already been taken."

"I know, but you know how we're going to do our project on this Icarus kid? Ms. Gilbert told me a little about him. He and his dad built these cool wings and then flew out of a maze."

"Icarus?" Alex said.

"Yeah. I looked online a little bit tonight before supper, and I couldn't find any spaceships or planes or anything named after Icarus."

"I guess it sounds cool, but I still think a girl's name would be better."

"Naw," Brian said. "Girls' names are no good for flying. You never hear about girl pilots. Just that one woman, what was her name? Amelia Earhart."

"Okay, *Icarus* it is." Alex patted the wing. "Hear that, *Icarus*? You've got a name now, so make us proud. Fly like you flew out of that maze."

They were so high now that Riverside resembled a little island of lights in a dark ocean. Cars and trucks driving on the streets looked like toys. Brian looked up and saw Mr. Piggly carrying them up into the sky. He swallowed. How high was five thousand feet? He had seen videos on the Internet where cameras tied to balloons soared up practically to space. On one, the camera picked up the curvature of the earth.

Brian shivered. Was it getting colder or was he just scared? If they went up too high, they'd start to run out of oxygen. Then there was a lot of stuff about air currents that he didn't understand. If they flew into one of those, they could be blown hundreds of miles away.

"Alex, check the gauge. How high are we?"

"Just a little higher to go. This thing's reading four thousand eight hundred thirteen feet."

"Does that mean four thousand eight hundred feet above sea level or four thousand eight hundred feet above the ground?"

Alex didn't answer right away. "Oh . . . um, I don't know. I never thought about that. I wish we could ask Max. He'd know."

Brian remembered that when he used to fly with Dad, he would check the altimeter and then look out the window to see how small houses and cars appeared at different altitudes. The houses were tiny now, but he had no idea how high they were.

"We're at five thousand feet now," said Alex.

"I don't think we should wait any longer. It's time to start the engine."

"Woo-hoo! Fire this baby up! Let's go, *Icarus*! It's flying time."

"Okay, don't kick the pins out until I tell you to. I have to start the engine and get our speed up first."

"You got it!"

When Brian leaned forward to grab the handle on the engine's pull-start rope, *Icarus* rocked in her cables a little, just enough to make his stomach twist around. He wasn't afraid of heights, he reminded himself. He was only afraid of being really high up on something shaky and unstable. He got a hold of the handle and yanked. The engine sputtered and growled a bit, but then died down.

"Come on, *Icarus*. Fire up, baby!" Alex shouted.

Brian pulled even harder. *Icarus* rocked some more, but the engine didn't engage. Brian pulled again. No good. He took the handle with both hands and tugged as hard as he could, again and again and again. *Icarus* swung back and forth under Mr. Piggly.

"Whoa," Alex said. "We're really shaking here. Is there a problem?"

What if the engine didn't start at all? How would they get back down? They didn't have any parachutes. There was no backup plan. Once they had the engine going, they were just supposed to fly under their own power until they came in for a safe landing.

"Please, baby. You gotta start," Brian whispered. He pulled the starter again. The engine roared to life, propeller spinning.

Suddenly, something somewhere cracked, and *Icarus* lurched hard to the left, dropping its right wing almost straight down. Alex screamed behind him. Brian grabbed on to the port-side wing and looked back. The rope tying the right side of the aircraft to the balloon had already come loose somehow. Alex had fallen out of his seat, but managed to grab the right-side skateboard. He kicked his legs in the open air beneath him. "Brian, help! I'm gonna fall!"

What could he do? There was only one safe way back down. Struggling to hold on, Brian slammed the throttle lever up to give the engine more power. They shot forward, but with tethers holding only the front and left points of the aircraft, *Icarus* was almost totally on its side. Worse, while Brian could still pull the front pin to cut them loose from Mr. Piggly, there was no way Alex could reach the left-side pin now — not when he was struggling just to hang on.

"Brian! The tail's on fire!"

He glanced back. The rudder and horizontal stabilizer looked fine. "What do you mean?"

"Mr. Piggly!" Alex tried to kick a leg up to get back into the flyer. They lurched again. "His tail is on fire! The metal ring for the cable must have sparked when it broke."

Brian looked up. Alex was right. The dopey curly tail was burning, with bright red flames inching closer and closer to Mr. Piggly's butt. "The hydrogen!" Brian shouted. If the fire reached the balloon, all the gas inside it would ignite.

"That's going to be the biggest pig fart Riverside's ever seen!"

Brian pushed the throttle, trying to do something to save the situation while still holding on with one hand and squeezing the center plank between his legs to keep himself from falling. He was helpless unless he could get those other two pins pulled at the same time. If he pulled the front pin first, *Icarus* would tip straight down. They might be completely banked with one wing pointed to the ground right now, but at least the engine and tail were still on the same level.

"It's going to blow!" Alex kicked his legs again. Brian could see his arms shaking in the growing light from the burning tail. "We're going to die!"

WHOOF. Flames suddenly burst from the pig's butt and expanded fast. For an instant, Mr. Piggly's big grin stretched and his eyes grew wider, as if he was shocked at what was happening to him.

Then his face was all fire, and they were falling.

The wind whipped through Brian's hair. Somehow he managed to crank the yoke to the left and shift the ailerons into position. The whole aircraft shook. Brian could barely hold the yoke. But it worked! *Icarus* leveled out!

"Alex! I think I've got it! Hold on!"

"The heck you think I'm doing back here?" Alex screamed.

When the wings were level with the ground, Brian quickly pushed the yoke to starboard to flatten the ailerons, then moved it backward to try to bring the nose up. They were still plummeting down toward the darkness of the woods that lined the river, but the angle of their fall gradually flattened out as they shot forward. Mr. Piggly was nothing more than a big lump of burning rubber now, a fireball chasing them through the dark.

"Hold on, Alex!" If they hadn't dropped so fast at first, they'd be flying fine by now. In the dim light cast by the fire behind them, Brian could see tree branches to the right and left. They were over the river, and it was coming up fast.

"Brian!" Alex screamed as his grip on *Icarus* slipped. He fell away into the dark.

"Alex!" Brian pulled back on the yoke, trying to bring *Icarus* up. "Alex!"

Icarus's descent slowed until it was just above the surface of the river. "Come on, girl, pull up. Pull up," Brian muttered. The wheels skimmed the water with a little splash. He felt her slow down on contact. Then the skateboards entered the water too and he was thrown forward in his seat, just before the engine splashed down and water careened up to knock him out of the flyer. The cold water shot up his nose and into his mouth, and his face smacked the tail rudder as he somersaulted past it.

When he finally found which way was up, he surfaced and coughed out the river water. A smoky mess floated past him, the remains of that stupid pig balloon. A few feet downstream, *Icarus* floated on its Plastisteel wings.

"Alex!" Brian shouted, still hacking water as he swam after the flyer. "Alex!"

He grabbed hold of the flyer and kicked to push her onto the muddy shore. He scrambled up to the bank himself, then flopped over on his back in the muck, his eyes stinging. "Alex," he mumbled. How high had they been when Alex fell? What if they hadn't been over the river? Alex could have hit a tree or the ground, and even if he fell into the water, there were still branches and rocks. . . . "Oh, God, no, Alex."

"Brian?" A voice came from upstream. "Are you okay?"

Brian shook his head to try to get the water out of his ears. He couldn't have really heard what he thought he heard. "Alex?"

"Brian, where are you?"

They kept calling out to each other until Alex swam up beside him. Then they both staggered away from the river, over to a tree, and rested. They yelled to Max until he came running out of the scrub brush nearby.

"Are there any injuries?"

"I'm not broken," Alex said. "But that was the worst belly flop I've ever done."

Brian touched his puffy, sore cheek. "I think I'm okay."

Max dropped down to his knees, took off his glasses, and rubbed the bridge of his nose. "I saw the fireball and assumed the worst. What happened up there?"

"The engine wouldn't start," said Brian. "I had to keep pulling the starter cable, and that rocked us around a lot."

"Then one of the rings on Mr. Piggly broke and started the stupid balloon on fire," Alex said. "We were hanging there tipped on our side and I fell off."

Max closed his eyes, rested his chin on his chest, and let out a long breath. "It was great to hear you yelling to each other. You are very fortunate that you went down over the river." He was quiet for a moment. Then he took another deep breath, put his glasses back on, stood up, and walked toward *Icarus* on the bank. "How's the flyer?"

"She was flying, Max," Brian said. "If she would have had a more controlled drop, if we would have had just a little more time to level out, I swear she would have pulled out of the fall."

Max examined the aircraft. "We'll need to get it back to the Eagle's Nest and check it under better light to be sure, but there doesn't appear to be any damage."

"A waterlogged engine, though." Alex coughed. "Maybe *Icarus* wasn't the luckiest name."

"You named the flyer *Icarus*?" Max asked.

"Ms. Gilbert talked about it," Brian said. "We thought it would be cool."

"Did either of you actually take the time to *read* the story of Icarus and Daedalus?"

Brian shook his head.

"The end of the Icarus story is that he flies too close to the sun, his wings melt and burn, and he crashes and drowns in the ocean."

"So the flyer needs a new name," Brian said. "And a new takeoff plan."

The next morning, Brian's mouth watered at the smell and sound of hot sizzling bacon. But he stopped when he entered the kitchen, surprised to find Grandpa and not Dad at the stove.

"Morning, sport!" Grandpa said. "You're just in time. Got some bacon and home-fried potatoes for you. I remember how you hate eggs." He placed a plate on the table and pulled out a chair. "Have a seat."

Brian sat down. It was true. He couldn't stand eggs. Something about that whole gooey glob of yellow pre-baby-chicken slime thing made him want to throw up. He just wished Grandpa had made this awesome breakfast another day when he didn't have this huge bruise on his face. He tried to keep Grandpa from getting a good look at him.

Brian ate in silence while Grandpa cleaned up the kitchen. It was a much better breakfast than his usual cereal.

"What are you doing here?" he finally said, finishing up the last of his food.

Grandpa groaned as he sat down across the table with a mug of steaming coffee in hand. "Truck's in the shop and I got a doctor's appointment at the V.A. in Iowa City. Your mother's going to drive me there on . . ." He peered closely at Brian. "Her way to . . . work."

Grandpa put his coffee down. The thud of the mug on the table echoed in the quiet kitchen. "Let me see your face."

Caught. He couldn't hide it now. Brian showed him as directed. "It's no big deal, really."

"No big deal." Grandpa's chair scraped the floor as he pushed it back. "I think you better come with me."

Brian wondered why adults bothered to say things like, "I think you better" as if it mattered if he thought differently. They really just meant, "Do whatever I'm about to tell you to do." He followed his grandfather out onto the back porch.

It was a cool morning, but sunny and bright. Grandpa reached into his pocket and pulled out a small brown cigar. Then he opened the top on his metal lighter and flicked the flame to life. He lit the cigar, and after a few puffs, he lowered it and tapped some ashes to the ground. "Brian, you may think I'm too ancient to understand much about what you're going through, but this old man is sharper than you know." His shoes clomped as he crossed the wooden floor. He took another drag on his cigar. "You've been into some trouble after school. Coming home with all these scrapes and bruises. I know what you've been up to."

Brian felt cold. Grandpa must have seen them bringing the flyer back to the Eagle's Nest last night. Now he'd tell Mom and Dad, and everybody would know about the stolen Plastisteel. He'd be grounded for the rest of his life and he'd never get the chance to fly. "I'm sorry," Brian said.

"Hold on." Grandpa had been smoking and looking out over the yard. Now he faced Brian again. "I know I made you promise to stay out of trouble, and I'm sure you tried." He pointed his cigar at Brian. "But sometimes trouble finds you, and it's not your fault."

What? How could working on the flyer in the Eagle's Nest possibly not be his fault?

"You got some guy thinks he's tough. Coming around making life hard, picking on you." Grandpa took a long drag. Brian felt relieved that he hadn't discovered the Eagle's Nest. A moment later Grandpa blew out smoke. "And I appreciate you trying to be good like I asked you to, but Brian, sometimes the only thing these tough guys understand is toughness. You sock him a good one" — he punched the air — "be amazed at how quick this so-called tough guy will fall. How quick he'll leave you be." He stabbed his cigar into the dirt in a flowerpot, then he waved his hand back and forth to shoo away the smoke. "Don't tell your mother I've been smoking out here. Okay, sport?"

Grandpa had his secrets too. "No problem," said Brian.

"And you think about what I told you," Grandpa said. He patted Brian on the shoulder as he went back inside.

Later, as he skated to school, Brian considered Grandpa's words. There were just two problems with the whole fight-back-against-Frankie thing. First, for a tough guy, Frankie was *really* tough. Sometimes in gym class, before Mr. Darndall even had them do anything, Frankie would knock out push-ups for no reason, sometimes over a hundred.

The second problem rolled up next to him just as his iPod switched to the Beatles' song "Getting Better." Brian popped out his earbuds, careful to keep the bruised side of his face away from her. "Hey, Wendy," he said.

"What? No half-pipe this morning?" she said.

"I don't think I could handle it today."

"Oh." She was quiet for a moment. "Hey, do you think you could give me a few pointers sometime?"

"Um, I don't know. Maybe." He sounded like an idiot.

"We could meet at the skate park tonight." She kicked up her speed a little. "Or, you know, we could get ice cream too."

One thing Brian knew about his life in Iowa so far was that everything could change very quickly. Last night he was miserable after crashing the flyer into the muck again. Now he almost felt like he could fly all on his own. He smiled so much that it hurt his bruised face. Without thinking, he reached up to touch his swollen eye.

"Wait. Are you okay?" Wendy asked.

Oh no. He kicked the ground to speed away from her.

"Brian," she said, "let me see your face."

"It's cool. Don't worry about it," said Brian.

"Come on. Show me. You can't hide all day."

"Fine." He looked at her.

Wendy gasped. "Oh my gosh. What happened?"

What could he say? Even if he could tell her about the flyer, she'd never believe him. "It's, um . . . hard to explain."

"It was Frankie, wasn't it?"

"No!" Brian objected so forcefully that he almost fell off *Spitfire*.

"Don't try to cover for him, Brian. I know he's been giving you crap."

The one time Frankie was innocent was when Wendy had to drag him into the situation. "It's nothing."

"It is *not* nothing!" Wendy shouted. They were starting down the Lincoln Street hill to the school, speeding up. It was usually a fun slope, but today she just stood straight up on her board with her arms folded. "I will *kill* him!"

"No, Wendy. Please. Trust me on this. He didn't do anything this time! It would be better if you didn't —"

"It would be better if my stupid brother left people alone!" Wendy kicked up a wicked ollie off the street onto the sidewalk in front of the school. Brian went to follow, but was distracted enough to hook his wheels on the curb. He stumbled, but caught himself just in time. Picking up *Spitfire*, he watched Wendy vanish into the school.

There were still twenty minutes until the first bell, but kids were already hanging out in the hallway or in groups around their desks. After stowing *Spitfire* in his locker and getting his books, Brian went to his seat between Alex and Max in homeroom.

Alex turned around and bit his lower lip. "I hurt everywhere. Who knew water could be so painful?"

Max spoke quietly. "I'm very pleased that you and Alex made it through last night's malfunction safely."

"I wouldn't call it safe," Brian said. "But at least we weren't killed."

Max smiled. "I have heard the expression, 'Any landing you can walk away from is a good landing.'"

"Any landing you can *swim* away from," Brian said.

Alex laughed a little. "Max, tell him."

"I remained in the Eagle's Nest late last night, checking over the damage. The flyer held together perfectly. The engine will have to be flushed and cleaned, but other than that, it should be as functional as it was before."

Which wasn't that great, Brian thought.

"What he means is that we're still in business," Alex said. "But just like before, we need to work on fixing up the engine and figuring out a new takeoff plan. So, Eagle's Nest. After school."

Brian shrugged. If Wendy hadn't freaked out about his

bruises, they could be skating together after school. He tried not to think about it.

It was almost a relief when Ms. Gilbert started class — that is, until she started them on their group projects. He'd had about all he could handle of stupid Icarus.

Frankie slammed Brian with the usual shoulder bumps after class. He left him alone the rest of the day, but Brian didn't want to take any chances with him after school. "Max," he said as they gathered up their books after the last bell, "do you want to go to the Eagle's Nest now? We could take the other way out of here."

Max nodded.

Outside, they crossed the playground and reached the big maple in the corner by the back fence. "You go first and then I'll toss our bags over," Brian said to Max.

Max went around the tree to the side with the low branch — then came flying back, landing on his butt. Frankie jumped out from behind the tree. He ran his hand through his curly black hair. "It took a little time to figure out how you two losers were always getting away after school, but I found your sissy escape path." He cracked his knuckles. That twitch was back in his eye, now focused on Brian. "Wendy says you've been going around telling everyone I beat you up."

"I did not."

Frankie shrugged. "I told her she was crazy. I told her I barely touched you in a long time. She didn't believe me."

Brian's legs shook. Max stood up next to him, but there was no rocketbike for their escape today.

Frankie gave Brian a quick shove in the chest. He was forced back a little. Grandpa wanted him to fight this guy? Maybe he could. Brian tightened his fist.

Frankie stretched his neck to one side and then the other. "Now, I told you not to talk to my sister, but you wouldn't listen." He shrugged and took another step closer. "And I figure since she's going to be mad at me for beating you up anyway, I might as well actually do it."

Max held up a hand. "There's no reason for this —"

Frankie shoved Max back. Brian rushed at Frankie, but he was too quick, slamming his fist into Brian's stomach. Brian bent over in pain, the wind knocked out of him.

"Just leave us alone!" Max shouted.

Frankie planted one boot behind Max's foot and pushed him back, dropping him on his butt. Brian tried to stand upright so he could punch Frankie in the face, but he couldn't breathe. Frankie grabbed him by the shirt and slung him into the fence. He hit the wood face-first and fell to the ground.

Frankie leaned down over him. He pounded his fist into his other hand. "See you tomorrow."

Then Brian and Max were alone on the quiet playground. A breeze blew over them, and from somewhere came the sound of the metal hook for the tetherball, clinking against the pole. Brian just stayed on the ground. He might never get up. Every time he tried, he came crashing back to the dirt again.

Then Max was above him, holding out a hand. "Let me help you up."

When Brian was on his feet, brushing himself off and feeling his stinging eye and cheek, Max handed him his backpack. "Come on," he said. "It makes no sense to take the secret way home now."

Neither of them spoke all the way across town to Grandpa's farm.

In the Eagle's Nest, it didn't take long for Max to disassemble the whole engine. He picked up a toothbrush and started scrubbing down some of the parts.

"Think you can fix this?" Brian asked.

"Most likely." Max put one part down and picked up another. "I don't think there is much damage. The engine parts will just have to be cleaned and lubricated."

"Anything I can do to help?" Brian looked over the mess of parts on the table.

Max pointed to the engine parts, bottles of water, brushes, and clean rags. "You can scrub down the components that are dusty from where the muddy water dried on them."

"I have my iPod," Brian said. "Music?" Max nodded, and Brian plugged his iPod into the speakers, putting on the Beatles' *White Album*.

They cleaned parts for a while, and nobody spoke. It was nice, just enjoying the music safe inside the Eagle's Nest. Except for the sting in his face, Brian could almost forget about Frankie.

After a long time, Max looked up from his work. "About this afternoon with Frankie . . . Thanks for trying to help. I'm sorry that —"

"Guys!" Alex shouted from the hole in the floor. "Check this out! I ordered it a long time ago, but it finally came today." He came up into the room and rushed to the table with a box so big it barely fit through the tunnel, but he stopped when he saw Brian's eye. "Whoa. Is your face actually getting worse? What happened?"

"Frankie," Brian said.

Alex stared at them both for a moment. "Yeah. Well . . . Hey! Check this out, check this out!" He put the box down on the east-side workbench and opened it. "Okay, so everybody's a little down about our second crash. I get it, but I have something here that might cheer you up."

He pulled out a big green metal box. It was the size and shape of a video-game console, but instead of a disc slot on the front, it had a bunch of knobs. Alex took out a long, narrow, folding metal strap and screwed it into the end with the knobs. Then he plugged in what looked like an antique telephone handset.

"It's a radio communication set," Max said.

"It's not just any old radio!" Alex answered. "This is the PRC-77, a retired military radio. This sucker can take a hit and keep on rolling." He reached into the box and pulled out another identical unit. "These things usually cost a fortune on eBay, but I've been looking all over the Internet and at military surplus stores and stuff, and you'll never believe this. Both radios, with batteries, antennae, and handsets, and I got the whole thing for, like, two hundred bucks!"

"You had two hundred dollars?" Brian asked.

"I called in a lot of bets and used savings from my birthday and stuff." Alex shrugged. "My point is, guys, now we can have a radio on the ground with Max and another up in the flyer. When the flyer is finally airborne, Max will be able to direct us around for all the cameras and stuff."

"If we can get this thing to fly," Max said.

Alex put his arm around Max's shoulders. "Of course we can get it to fly! I just spent two hundred bucks on radio equipment that says we can fly. You guys each take a radio home. Test them out. You'll love them. Now all we have to do is rework the engine. And we already have it all taken apart to do that."

Listening to him, Brian started to believe in the flyer again too. They had been close, after all. The first takeoff was almost a success, and the balloon plan might have worked if they had been able to have a controlled release.

"Come on, Max," Alex said. "You're a genius. I know you got some magic left in you to fix up this engine."

Max looked doubtful. "I suppose I could —"

"Yes! We're back in business," Alex said. "And you know what else the flyer needs? A name. A good name this time."

"How about Kendra?" Brian said. "You said it has to be a girl's name."

Alex rubbed his knuckles on his chin. "Tempting, but I was thinking —" He slapped his hands down on the center table. "Guys! Seriously! Why do we always have to play this Stone Age music?" He pulled his own iPod from his bag and went toward the speakers.

Max shook his head. "Just leave it! We always listen to what you want to hear. We do whatever you want to, just because you think you know what's cool. What makes your stuff so great? So superior? Just because it came out in the last two weeks! And what will happen two weeks from now?" Alex opened his mouth to speak, but Max held his hand up. "I'll tell you! In two weeks the song you're about to play right now will be old and everyone will say it's crap. Why? Because it really is crap!"

Nobody moved for a moment. Brian caught Alex's glance. Alex put his iPod down. "Wow. Dude, chill. It's okay. We can listen to —"

"He's right," Brian said.

In the silence, the song on the *White Album* changed to "Blackbird."

"I know you guys are upset about whatever Frankie did tonight, but don't take it out on me. What did I —"

"This is it!" Brian said.

"What is?" Alex asked.

Brian smiled. "Oh, it's perfect. 'Blackbird.'" He restarted the song so they could listen to the words.

> *Blackbird singing in the dead of night*
> *Take these broken wings and learn to fly*
> *All your life*
> *You were only waiting for this moment to arise*
>
> *Blackbird singing in the dead of night*
> *Take these sunken eyes and learn to see*
> *All your life*
> *You were only waiting for this moment to be free.*

Brian looked at Alex. "You said the flyer needs a new name. It's right in this song. All that stuff about waiting for this moment. About being free. About flying! Don't you see?"

"About fixing broken wings." Max took off his glasses and chewed on the earpiece.

Brian nodded. "We'll call her *Blackbird.*"

Alex patted the wing. "There's nothing black about it. It's bright white."

"I believe that's what they call irony," Max said.

"And the song is on the White *Album*, get it?" Brian said.

"No," Alex said. "I don't get it."

"Who votes to call her *Blackbird*?" Brian said. He raised his hand. Max raised his too.

Alex shrugged. "Okay. You win. *Blackbird* it is. It'll fly soon enough."

They worked for a long time that night, listening to some more Beatles for Brian, and even some Weird Al after Max asked for it. They drank soda until the twenty-four pack was nearly empty. By the time they were done, the engine was perfectly clean and reassembled.

"Well," Max said. "*Blackbird* is restored. It's ready for another trial run."

Brian thought late into the night. Ever since Frankie had messed up Brian's first day on the half-pipe here in Riverside, he had been trying to fly, but crashing. With the flyer, with the guys at school, or with Wendy, as soon as things were looking up, everything went right back down. Grandpa's advice to fight Frankie had resulted not only in Brian breaking his promise to Wendy, but also a complete disaster. Now Brian, like *Blackbird*, needed a new plan.

The next morning at school, he stowed his things in his locker and went into homeroom. Wendy sat at her desk, with Abbie, Jess, Heather, and Rowena circled around her as usual. Brian sighed. Maybe he could talk to Wendy later. He started down the row to his desk, but he stopped when he heard Frankie's loud voice from out in the hallway.

No. He had to do this before he chickened out.

He put his books down on his desk and turned around. Maybe talking to a girl was a lot like flying a plane. The toughest part was getting started in the first place. And there was only one way to take off successfully. Fast.

Brian marched right up to the Wolf Pack. "Wendy Heller."

Heather leaned in to whisper something in Jess's ear. They both giggled.

"Hey, Brian," Wendy said.

"Let's talk," Brian said. "Maybe in the hallway?"

Wendy stood up. "Sure." People in the room went "oooh" or made kissing noises as he led her to the hallway, checking first to make sure Frankie had moved on.

"What's up?" she said when they were outside the classroom door.

Brian's hands were damp and his heartbeat heavy. He faced this most beautiful girl. "Yesterday you asked if we should . . . er . . . if it would be cool if . . . you know." He stopped and took a breath. Captain Kirk was never nervous around the ladies on *Star Trek*. He put on his best Captain Kirk smile. "Would you like to meet me at the skate park after school?"

"Really?"

Brian nodded. "Really. It'll be fun. I'll teach you some moves."

Wendy dropped her gaze to the floor. "No, Brian. I don't think so."

He instantly wanted to run all the way home — his old

home in Seattle. "Oh," he said. "Sure. I get it. No problem. I just thought —"

"Because *I'm* the one who's going to teach *you* tricks." Wendy's grin was big and beautiful. She laughed a little. "Got you! The skate park at four thirty, then." She did the whole teeny-tiny wave thing and spun around to go back into the room.

Brian found it difficult to focus on his schoolwork that morning. He couldn't stop thinking about his upcoming time with Wendy. During group work in language arts, Alex had to tell him to stop smiling so much.

He was feeling so good that by lunchtime, he figured he'd try to sit at the cool table again. When they were dismissed for lunch, Max started to ask Brian if he wanted to eat with him, but Brian pretended he hadn't heard. He didn't stall with Ms. Gilbert as he often did, but darted out of his seat and slipped around two people in his own row to get out the door first. In the cafeteria, he was near the front of the line for a change, and he took his tray with chicken nuggets, green beans, a stale cookie, and milk straight to the table where Alex, Red, David, and the other cool guys usually sat. He sat down, trying to act natural, like this was no big deal.

Red and David took seats across from him. Red looked at Brian for a moment and then opened his mouth and let out a long rippling belch. Brian and David laughed.

"That's how he says hello," said David.

Alex slid onto the bench next to Brian. "I heard that burp, dude," he said to Red. "That was a long one." Timmy Hale and Kevin Stein from the other sixth grade class joined them. Dakota Smith and Travis Jacobs were next.

The table was full, and no Frankie.

"Yeah? You think that's a long belch?" Red pointed at Alex with one of his chicken nuggets. "When my dad was in the Air Force —"

"Was that before he worked for the CIA?" David asked.

"And before he worked for the county like he does now?" said Kevin.

If Red picked up on the disbelief, he didn't act like it. "Yeah, before he worked for the county. Anyway, when he was a fighter pilot in the Air Force, he used to get this special soda that they only give to pilots. You know, scientific stuff that helps keep them awake on long flights. Well, I drank, like, a whole can of it in about thirty seconds, even though the warning label said not to drink it that fast. I let out this one burp and it lasted over two minutes straight." Red looked around the table. "I'm serious. I almost passed out."

"Red said!" David shouted. Everybody burst out laughing. Some milk shot out of Timmy's nose.

"Red said!" Alex yelled.

"Reeeeeed said!" Travis joined them.

Brian couldn't resist. "Red said!"

Red finally put the chicken nugget in his mouth. He talked while chewing. "Why don you guysh ever belee me?"

"Better question," a voice said right behind Brian. "What is this loser doing in my seat?"

Brian sat up straight. How did this guy always manage to sneak up and ruin everybody's good time?

Frankie tapped him on the shoulder. "Hey. You're in my seat."

Everybody at the table went quiet. Brian looked around for any adults. Mrs. Valentine had been on lunch-monitor duty, but she must have stepped out, and the lunch ladies were busy.

"So are you gonna get up and go sit with that dork Mad Max," Frankie said, "or am I going to have to force you to move?"

"What difference does it make?" Brian couldn't make himself face Frankie, but he could still talk to him. "It's just a seat."

Frankie didn't say anything for a minute. Alex, Red, David, and the others kept their eyes locked on their trays. "Come on, guys. I been sitting here all year. You can't just let this freak take my place," Frankie said. Nobody said a word. "Come on, Red. Tell him to move."

"Well, I don't know . . ." Red said.

"Alex," said Frankie. "Buddy. We go way back. We used to build snow forts together on the playground during kindergarten recess. Now you're letting this guy sit in my seat? You're not actually friends with this idiot, are you?"

"What?" Alex said. "I, uh . . ."

Brian felt something cold and wet on the back of his neck. He reached back and touched it, then looked at his fingers. They were dark red and dripping.

"What difference does it make?" Frankie said. "It's just barbecue sauce. Alex, check it out, the dork looks like he was shot in the back of the head. He's got barbecue-sauce blood oozing down his neck."

Alex actually made a little half laugh sound, but a couple of the other guys at the table shook their heads.

"See you around, Brian." Frankie stormed off. When Brian dared to look, he spotted Frankie sitting at a table with B.A. Pineeda, Chris Miller, and Jason Cooper.

Brian felt the barbecue sauce running down inside his shirt. He looked at Alex. Frankie had put him on the spot, and he had just stammered around, as helpless as Brian had been all the times before. Brian had thought Alex was so cool, that he always knew how to handle any situation. But how could a guy be even close to cool when he just abandoned a friend like that? What kind of guy let his friend get picked on?

Brian froze. Max sat alone, facing away from him at the other end of the cafeteria.

Yeah, what kind of guy?

He wanted to go to the bathroom to clean up, but then it would look like he was just running away. While the guys started a halfhearted discussion about football, he finished his chicken nuggets and took a bite out of his dried-out cookie. Then he got up from the table with his tray.

After school, Brian spotted Frankie in the crowd heading for the back door, maybe going to see if Brian was taking the old secret way. No problem. He hopped on *Spitfire* and rolled away from the front of the school.

He went home to drop off his books. A note on the fridge said he was supposed to be home by six for supper. He was about to head out again, but stopped just short of the front door. Wendy said to meet her at four thirty. It was just three thirty now, and it wouldn't do any good to be at the skate park too early.

More important, what if Wendy was thinking this whole skating thing was a date? How did anyone know they were on a date? Mom sometimes watched these terrible movies where a guy would ask a girl to dinner and then the girl would say yes. Then the guy would say "Great. It's a date." Brian had just said something like, "Do you want to go to the skate park?"

Maybe he should have said it was a date. Unless she didn't think this meeting was a big deal and would have laughed at him for thinking a girl like her would ever go out with someone like him. Brian sighed, pressed his hands to the sides of his head, and paced the kitchen.

He went to his room. The first thing he knew he had to do was get a clean shirt. He looked in his closet and pulled out his two best shirts, a white button-up and his cool Beatles T-shirt with the *Magical Mystery Tour* album cover printed on the front. How was he supposed to know what to wear?

The phone rang. It was probably Wendy calling to tell him she didn't want to meet with him, or Frankie saying he wasn't allowed to see her. Brian ran to the nearest handset. "Hello?"

"Brian?" It was Alex.

"Oh, hey." He wasn't at the top of the list of people Brian wanted to talk to.

"I'm sorry for what happened at lunch today. That was just stupid. I don't even know why I hang around with Frankie at all. I mean, I don't outside of school anymore, but in school . . . it's like I don't even choose who I get to hang around with."

Brian appreciated the apology, but he didn't really have time for what Alex was saying. "Yeah, well, I don't care about that right now."

"Well, what do you want me to do? I said I was sorry. I don't —"

"No, no. That's all fine." Brian leaned against the wall in the hallway. As much as he needed help, part of him also felt like he needed to keep this whole skating event or date thing a secret. On the other hand, Alex had been so smooth with Kendra. . . . Maybe he could help Brian out here.

"Then what, man?" Alex said. Brian didn't answer. "I was just about to head out to the Eagle's Nest. See you there?" Brian should just tell him. It was probably no big deal anyway. Nobody said anything for a moment. "Hello? You there?"

"No," Brian said.

"Wait. You're not there, or you're not going to the Eagle's Nest?"

"I need some advice." He told Alex about the skating plans with Wendy.

"Whoa . . . You're a legend. I wondered what you two were talking about this morning before school. And I've heard that Wendy might kind of like you."

"Might kind of like"? What did that mean? Still, Brian was happy to hear it. "So what should I do?"

"First," Alex said. "You don't have to say 'It's a date' for it to actually *be* a date."

"Yeah, I figured," Brian said.

"My older cousin in Lone Tree goes on dates with girls all the time and he just calls it 'watching movies.' You know what I mean?" Alex laughed.

Brian had no clue. "Yeah." He forced a little chuckle.

"Like he'll go down to the family room in the basement with a girl and they'll just *say* they're going to watch movies, but they don't do much watching."

What was Alex talking about? "So this thing tonight —"

"This is basically a date. You better not mess it up." Alex paused for a moment. "Oh! Do you have any cologne?"

"No," Brian said.

"Dude. Seriously."

"I mean, yeah, I have some. Or I used to have some." He'd never had any cologne. Why would he possibly want cologne? "A big bottle. But I think I might have used it all up back in Seattle."

"Oh, man. I bet Seattle girls rock."

"Yeah." Brian paced to the other end of his bedroom. "Plus, you know, it's a big city, so . . . there's lots of them."

"Okay, you need to hurry up and get ready for this. Take a shower. Brush your teeth. Use some mouthwash too. Then see if your dad has some cologne."

"This sounds really complicated," Brian said.

"Dude, I know! When you go on a date with a girl, it is complicated, believe me. You have to buy her something. Ice cream, or maybe some flowers."

"Really?"

"You didn't know that?" Alex said. "Seattle girls must be a lot different. You don't have much time, so listen. Have you heard of the yawn maneuver?"

"The what?"

Alex sighed. "Seriously. Okay, all you have to do to get things started is when you're sitting by her, you yawn and stretch your arms straight up. Then when you're done, instead of putting your arms back like normal, you slip your arm over her shoulder. She won't even realize your arm is around her. From there you can move on to other things."

What other things? They were just supposed to be meeting to skateboard.

"And watch for her signals."

"Signals?" Brian asked.

"Girls put out certain signals. Like, if she keeps looking down or away, that's because she's nervous about what she wore. She's wondering if she looks fat or whatever. If she does this, you have to compliment her. Tell her she smells good or something. If she's quiet for a real long time, like for almost a minute, if she kind of looks at you during that time, that means she wants you to kiss her. Then you know what to do."

"Yeah, I know," Brian said. He didn't know anything. Why couldn't two people just skate? Why did this have to be so complicated?

"Good luck," said Alex. "I expect a full report. I'm off to the Eagle's Nest."

They hung up. Brian showered, washing his hair twice with both shampoo and that conditioner stuff that was exactly like shampoo. When he was dressed in jeans and his white shirt with buttons and the annoying collar, he went back to the bathroom.

After brushing his teeth, he looked in the cabinet until he found the mouthwash that his father used. In the commercials, a guy always swished this stuff around in his mouth, and then some beautiful girl would put her arms around his shoulders and smile because his breath was so fresh. Brian poured some into the cap and then tipped it back.

It burned! His eyes watered while his mouth was on fire. Brian spat the mouthwash into the sink, turned on the water, and put his mouth under the faucet. He spat again. How could the guys on TV look so happy while they used this crap? He had to rinse and spit again and again to get the sick chemical taste out of his mouth. It was a battle to keep from throwing up.

When the mouthwash ordeal was finally over, Brian searched the bathroom cupboards for cologne. He thought he remembered Dad having some, but he hadn't ever paid too close attention to his father's bathroom stuff. Finally, he found it on the top shelf of a side cupboard, a small green bottle with a gold-colored cap and *Old World Fire* written in fancy gold letters on the front.

Brian took the cap off the bottle and sniffed the cologne. It was strong stuff. He'd just pour some on his hand and then put it on his neck. When he tipped the bottle, though, a lot of it poured out way too fast. He didn't need anywhere near that much. Dumping most of it out into the sink, he dabbed a little on his neck.

He sneezed. The smell was powerful. He put the cap back on the bottle and put the cologne away. That didn't make a difference. The smell was still *everywhere*.

Even with the bathroom fan on and the door open, the fragrance nearly made his eyes water. He scrubbed his hands with a ton of soap and the water as hot as he could stand it, but the cologne only backed off a little bit. He washed his hands again and then a third time.

Finally, Brian gave up. If he didn't get down to the skate park soon, he'd be late, and then all of this preparation would be for nothing. He looked himself over in the mirror one last time, then took a deep breath and spoke to his reflection. "Ready as you'll ever be."

When he rolled into the skate park, Wendy was perched with her board on the lip at the top of the half-pipe. She didn't seem to hear him coming, and Brian didn't call out to her. Her purple helmet caught a glint of sunlight as she looked at the ramp in front of her.

Then she put her foot on the raised front end of her board and rolled, skating smoothly all the way to the other lip where, after a kickturn, she rolled back down. The next part of the run was a little wobbly, and Wendy stomped the tail to bring her front trucks up, scraping to a stop on the flat. She took her helmet off and brushed her fingers through her long dark hair.

Wendy Heller was the most perfect girl in the universe, Brian thought. And now he might be on a date with her.

"Nice trick," he said. Wendy jumped, dropping her

helmet. It hit the metal ramp with a clang. He held his hands up. "Sorry."

Wendy shook her head. "I can't get it right. I could go back and forth probably all day if I rode back fakie, but I'm never going to get air in reverse."

"Your kickturn was good," he said. "But you're leaning the wrong way coming back down the ramp. You were sort of off to the side, and you need to get repositioned to lean into the roll on the way down."

Wendy folded her arms. "Can you show me?"

"I'll give it a try." He took *Spitfire* up on the platform of the half-pipe. "It's not just in how you move the board. You have to make sure your body is positioned right too." He launched himself down the ramp and skated back and forth from one platform to the other, building speed. Finally, when he rolled up on the other side and shot into the air, he reached back to grab *Spitfire* and yanked the board around in a good spin — too long maybe? He bent his knees to bring the board tighter to him.

He made the 360! The wheels slapped the ramp just in time to roll back down to the flat bottom. He jumped off and ran to a stop, spreading his arms wide in triumph. He'd totally just nailed the Ultimate Trick!

"Have you done that before?" Wendy clapped. "That was amazing."

"Yeah, I've . . ." His heart was pounding through his whole body. He took a deep breath to steady himself. "Done it all the time."

"You liar!" She laughed. "That was totally your first time. You're lucky you didn't fall on your butt."

"Okay," Brian said. "I've been trying to carve that trick for years. This was the first time I did it."

"What did you do different?" she asked.

He shrugged. "I don't know. Maybe you're my good-luck charm."

"Maybe I would be . . ." Wendy said, "if you didn't use such *terrible* lines!" She put her finger in her mouth, pretending like she was gagging.

Brian laughed. "Maybe we should try something easier for a while."

"Deal." She frowned and sniffed, then her eyes widened. "Brian, are you wearing cologne?" She tried to hide her giggle behind her hand.

"Um, no." He kicked *Spitfire* forward to hide his blush, heading toward a small ramp off to the side. "Just soap."

"You lie again!" Wendy laughed and skated after him. They skated all sorts of tricks, hitting some smaller ramps and jumping their boards up to grind on some low rails. Brian didn't worry about Frankie, or the Wolf Pack, or dates, or anything. He just skated and had fun. It was a lot like hanging out with Alex and Max in the Eagle's Nest, he thought. Only Wendy was beautiful, and she didn't belch like Alex or spout off super-complicated science stuff like Max. She was different. Special. She was . . . she was Wendy Heller.

When they were both pretty tired, they sat on a bench to rest for a minute. Brian wondered if Wendy's silence was one of the signals Alex had talked about. Then she stood up. "Come on," she said. "I want to show you something."

Brian would have followed her anywhere, but after they walked a couple blocks up to the square, he became curious. "Where are we going?"

She led him through the square and past the fountain in the middle of Carl Jacobs Park. They stopped outside a two-story red brick building. The year *1912* had been carved into a large stone block up near the roof in the middle of the storefront. A round sign painted to look like a clock swung in the breeze, squeaking on its rusted chains, with the words *Time Remembered* in fading letters at the center.

Wendy put her hand on the doorknob and glanced at Brian, but then quickly looked away. After a moment she opened the door. A bell jangled over their heads as they entered.

They stood in a crowded antique shop with almost too much to look at right at first. A blue glass ball lamp hung from a chain in the store window. Next to that stood a birdcage with chipped white paint. Shelves filled with old glasses and bottles lined the brick walls to the right and left. Some antique farm tools were mounted on the wall in one corner.

A few ancient-looking painted wood tables in the center held a jumble of other items.

"Hey, babe. Who's your friend?" A woman with brown curly hair pulled back into a ponytail came through a door at the back. She went behind a glass display case near the cash register.

"This is Brian Roberts," Wendy said.

"Roberts. Roberts. Hmm." The woman leaned over the counter and looked closely at him. "What's your mother's name?"

"Diane," said Brian.

"Diane Davis?" she asked. Brian nodded. She smiled. "Wow. I'd heard she was back in town! I'm Gwen Smith — Dakota's mom. I was in school with your mother. How do you like Riverside so far?"

Most of the time when adults asked how he liked something, they really just wanted him to say how good it was. Brian decided to be polite. "I really like it," he said. He looked at Wendy. Why had she brought him here? To introduce him to Dakota's mother?

"I know you're closing soon," Wendy said. "But I wanted to show Brian the book room."

"You want to take this boy upstairs?" The woman grinned.

Wendy's cheeks flared red. "Gwen!"

Gwen laughed and motioned toward the stairway. "I'm just kidding. Go ahead, and don't worry about closing time.

Stay as long as you like. I have some paperwork to catch up on anyway."

Brian followed Wendy up the wooden stairs to the second floor. Clothes racks displayed suits, dresses, jackets, and old shirts. Hats and ties dangled from hooks on the back wall. A few antique chandeliers hung from the ceiling, but Wendy switched them off. Plenty of light spilled across the floorboards through the three tall windows in the front. More shelves lined the brick walls on both sides, but these were packed with books.

"Gwen used to babysit Frankie and me sometimes," Wendy said. She went to stand by the windows, so Brian could only make out her silhouette against the bright sunlight. "When we were younger. A long time ago." From somewhere in the store came the sound of a ticking clock. She came away from the window and gave him a sad smile. "I used to play up here while Frankie would play in the courtyard or with some of the toys downstairs. I'd put on the dresses and pretend I was a princess locked away in a tower." She smiled. "One time Dakota tried to be a prince and rescue me. He found a metal helmet downstairs, and he came charging up with a yardstick for a sword and the lid from a skillet as his shield."

Brian sat down on a small cushioned wooden couch. "How did that go?"

"Frankie decided he'd play too. Only he was a robot, I think." She laughed. "He had one of those old-fashioned hand-crank mixer things and walked around saying 'Frank-O-Tron-5000-will-grind-your-face-off.' He kind of ruined it."

"He's good at that." Brian said the words before he realized that was probably a bad idea. Wendy froze. "I'm sorry," he said. "I didn't mean —"

"It's okay," she said. "I know. I know he's been mean. He wasn't always this way, you know. He used to be really nice. He still is nice to me, but . . . he's changed." She pulled a book from the shelf and flipped through its pages without seeming to look at it. "These last few years, I feel like I hardly know him sometimes. Now I come up here to hide out." She made a sweeping gesture with her arm. "All these old things. They weren't always forgotten junk. They used to belong to people, you know. They were Christmas and birthday presents. Wedding gifts."

Brian waited for her to go on. She was silent for a long time, but somehow he knew this wasn't one of the signals Alex had talked about. Finally, the quiet was uncomfortable. "Frankie's not that bad," he said.

Wendy nodded, but tears were in her eyes. She put the book back on the shelf. "I'm sorry," she said. "You don't want to hear about all this."

"No," he said. He couldn't stand to see her cry. How could he fix this? "I mean, whatever. It's cool."

She wiped her eyes. "Frankie was a really nice guy. Then, about two years ago, there was a bad snowstorm. Mom was on her way home from Iowa City." She breathed deeply. "It wasn't anybody's fault. Nobody to blame or anything. Just ice and snow and . . . a crash." She shrugged. "Mom was dead."

Brian had never known a kid his age with a parent who was dead. He wanted to help her, to do something or say something to make her less sad, but there was nothing he could do. "I'm sorry," he said. The words felt useless. He couldn't help her. Not really.

"It's a little easier to deal with now," she said. "Still, it's like the guys, the other girls, even the teachers just want me to move on and forget it." She wiped her eyes again. "Forget her. And at home it's just . . . Here in the store . . ." She pointed at the clothes in the back. "Where some of Mom's old things are for sale . . . I come up here and read or write in the quiet, and I feel like I don't have to forget. Time remembered, right?"

Neither of them spoke. The clock ticked.

"You're different than the others, Brian," Wendy said.

What did she mean by that? "Different bad or diff —"

"Different good. You're a good skateboarder. You're not a show-off like Alex or David or Red." Brian could feel his cheeks turning red. He wasn't used to getting compliments from a girl like Wendy. He didn't get very many compliments at all. "Thanks for coming here with me. I've never shown anyone my book room."

He felt good, closer to Wendy now that she had shared these secrets with him. He couldn't tell her about *Blackbird* or the Eagle's Nest, but he could share something to let her know he trusted her too. "Before I left my house today, Alex told me all these things I should do or say —"

Wendy giggled. "Oh no, did he tell you about his famous yawn maneuver?"

"What?" Brian said. How could she know about it? Had she and Alex dated?

"A bunch of us went to the movies last year. He had this big crush on Jess O'Claire, and he did this thing where he acted like he was yawning and stretching his arms, but then he put his arm around her like he was all smooth. She moved to a different seat."

Brian nodded. "What I mean is that, with you, I haven't had to worry about all that stuff Alex was talking about." He looked at her. "You're just . . . really great to talk to."

"Thanks," she whispered. "You too."

The quiet that followed somehow felt very different than it had a few moments ago. Brian pretended to read the spines of some of the books. Finally, he worked up the courage to say something. "Would you like to go get some ice cream?"

"Sure," she said.

He stood up, and they went back down the stairs and said good-bye to Gwen. The Tasty Freeze was too far away, so they picked up soft-serve cones at the gas station. Just like with the hot chocolate at the football game weeks ago, Brian felt really good buying something for Wendy, even if it was just something cheap. It made the whole afternoon feel more important somehow. More like a date, maybe.

They walked through town with their skateboards under their arms, licking their ice-cream cones. Wendy led the way to the railroad tracks and then headed south. She stopped in the middle of the bridge and sat on the limestone edge with her feet dangling.

Brian chuckled. "You sure aren't afraid of heights," he said. "It must be fifty feet down." He sat down beside her, but not too close. He didn't want to weird her out.

Her ice cream was down to just the cone. "Yuck," she said. She threw the cone off the bridge and it landed with a tiny splash in the gurgling water. "I hate the cone. It gets all soggy."

Brian actually liked eating the cone, but he dropped his off the edge as well, watching it tumble to its final plop. "I'd hate to fall off this thing."

"You mean *you're* afraid of heights?" Wendy said. She closed her eyes, seeming to enjoy the sun on her face and the breeze in her long hair.

"I'm not afraid of anything," Brian said.

"You liar." She opened her eyes, her smile fading to a serious expression. "I think you're afraid of my brother."

Brian looked away. He couldn't tell this girl that he sort of hated her brother.

"And maybe," she said, "you're still a little nervous about living in a completely new place."

"What?" he said. What was her deal? If he wanted to be called a coward, he'd go find Frankie. "I'm totally fine here."

"Yeah." Wendy moved closer to him on the bridge. "Me too." She watched him for a moment with those deep green eyes. Finally, she looked away. "They call this the Runaway Bridge," she said. "They say that a long time ago, like in the sixties or seventies, these two kids were in love, only the girl's father didn't want her to be dating her boyfriend. One day the boy was over at her house. He was supposed to leave before the father got home from work, but on that day, the girl's dad showed up early. The boy and girl weren't doing anything, just talking. But the dad went crazy and threatened to beat the boy up. He chased him out of the house and kept after him for blocks and blocks."

She stopped for a moment. Then she slid her hand toward him. Brian's heart beat heavier as her fingertips brushed his. Somehow their fingers interlocked and fit perfectly. Her hand was soft and warm, and he rubbed her thumb with his.

"The father couldn't keep up with the boy, so the boy got away. He ran down the slope and hid on a sandbar under this railroad bridge. The girl was furious at her father and worried about her boyfriend, so she ran away and met her boyfriend here at the bridge.

"Some say they left town together that day — ran away and never came back. Others believe that she eventually went home, but from that day on, whenever they wanted to be together, they'd run away to this bridge."

"Which story do you believe?" Brian asked.

She looked serious. "It depends on the day," she said. "And how I feel."

She didn't look away. She squeezed his hand, and he squeezed back. Then she moved closer. He wanted to kiss her, but he'd never kissed a girl before. What was he supposed to do? Hoping he'd get this right, he leaned toward her.

"MAD MAX! Get back here!" Frankie's voice echoed through the woods. "Don't think you can get away!"

Max came bursting out of some shrubbery at the top of the ridge, just before the ground sloped down to the river, less than a hundred yards downstream from the bridge. Frankie followed a few paces behind.

"Oh no," Wendy groaned.

"I have to go help him." Brian let go of her hand and stood up. Then he ran off toward the slope.

"Wait!" Wendy was right behind him.

He ran as fast as he could along the top of the ridge, cutting through scrub brush and ducking under a few low-lying tree branches. Frankie had caught Max by the shirt, stopping him about six feet down from the top of the ridge. When he saw Brian, he put on his evil grin.

"Just who I was looking for," Frankie said. He shoved Max hard, sending him sliding and rolling down the hill until he splashed into the English River.

"Knock it off, Frankie!" Wendy shouted behind Brian. "Why do you have to be like this?"

"Oh, and this dork is here in the woods with my sister!" He tapped at his temple and pointed at Brian. "Hmm. I seem to remember telling you not to even talk to Wendy."

"I can do what I want!" Wendy said.

"You can. Yes," Frankie said. "But he can't." He grabbed Brian's arms and twisted him to throw him like he'd done to Max.

"No way, man." Brian gritted his teeth and gripped Frankie's arms, pushing back.

"Stop it, you two!" Wendy tried to pull them apart. "Just leave each other alone!"

"No problem," Frankie said. He stepped backward, throwing Brian off balance. Before Brian could figure out what to do, Frankie planted a foot behind his and pushed him back, sending him flailing through the air.

Brian hit the dirt on his back, rolled up and over, scraped through a prickly bush, and then splashed down in the cold river. He took in a mouthful of muddy water and stood up coughing. Before the water was out of his eyes, he felt a hand on his shoulder. He cocked back his fist, ready to fight.

"Brian, it's me!" Max said just in time.

Brian checked his punch and wiped his face. He slipped in the mud and fell down on his belly in the water again.

"Let me go, Frankie!" Wendy's voice echoed down the slope. She struggled to get out of her brother's grip. "Brian, I'll call you!"

"You will not!" Frankie said.

Brian crawled up on the muddy riverbank and rolled over onto his back. Max collapsed next to him. He listened to the sound of Wendy and Frankie's argument fading as they walked farther and farther away.

After a long time, Brian asked, "What is that guy's problem?"

"In general, I believe Frankie's a little overprotective of Wendy due to his feelings of insecurity after the loss of his mother."

Brian stared at the tree branches above him. "You got that from a book."

"It's a theory," Max said. "I was on my way from the Eagle's Nest to buy some soda tonight when Frankie started chasing me. He was convinced I knew where you were. I did know because Alex had told me, but for the record, I did not tell Frankie that you were on a date with Wendy. How did that go, anyway?"

"Great." Brian smiled, remembering the perfect afternoon with Wendy. Then he spat to try to get the dirty water taste out of his mouth, thinking of how Frankie had ruined it all again. "Just great."

After a soggy walk home, Brian sneaked up the stairs to the back porch, knowing he was probably late for supper. It would have been okay with him to be late because of Wendy, but he hated the idea of getting in trouble thanks to Frankie. And no matter what, Mom and Dad would be furious if they saw him this dirty.

Lights were on in the kitchen. That meant at least one of his parents was home.

"You are being ridiculous about this!" Mom's shout sounded through the porch windows.

"It's only temporary," Dad said. "We'll pay him back. Your father says he wants to help."

Brian leaned his head against the outside of the house. They were both home, and they were not happy.

"He's already letting us live here rent-free," Mom said. "You want to ask for more?"

"This isn't my fault! We wouldn't have to do this if that first batch of Plastisteel hadn't been stolen." Brian lightly thumped his head against the house. "Anyway, I don't see what the big deal is," Dad said. "Mary has asked —"

"You know, I am getting just a little bit tired of hearing about *Dr. Warrender* and how great she is."

"Are you kidding me? You're *still* jealous?"

Now was as good a time as any to sneak in. He could get inside and get up to his bedroom to change before he was noticed. Quiet was the key. He gripped the doorknob and turned it all the way before pulling the door open. It would start to creak if he moved it past the halfway point, so he only cracked it a little bit before squeezing in through the gap.

"What on earth happened to you?" Mom said. Brian jumped. She was right in front of him. "Brian, you're filthy! What were you doing?"

"Mom, it's not my fault. I was just —"

"Is that your new shirt? The nice shirt I bought for you to wear to your father's big dinner with Mrs. Douglas?" She grabbed his sleeve. "It's ruined!"

Dad came into the kitchen. "What's going on?" He saw Brian. "You're late. Didn't you read the note? What have you been doing?"

"Brian, why were you even wearing this shirt?" Mom asked.

"Who were you with?" Dad asked.

It was one of very few nights when both Mom and Dad were home for supper together. Now they were just going to yell at him?

"Brian, answer us," Mom said.

"Nothing!" Brian said. How could he tell them? They'd never understand about Frankie, and he certainly wasn't going to tell them about Wendy. "I wasn't doing anything!"

"Oh, really?" Dad said. "Good. Well, you'll be doing a lot more nothing in the future. You are grounded! From now on, one of us will be calling the house at three thirty. That will give you half an hour to get home after school. If you're not here to answer the phone, I'll start assigning extra punishments."

"It's not my fault! You can't just —"

"I have too much going on to deal with crap like this, Brian. This is a critical time for Synthtech. I need you to do your part to help."

After Brian showered and changed clothes, they ate their hamburgers and fries in silence, and then he went to his room. At first he paced the floor, mad about having been grounded, furious at Frankie for ruining the perfect day. He tried using the PRC-77 radio that he'd brought home days ago to connect with the one Max had. He keyed the handset. "Anyone there?" Nothing. He went back to pacing. Since moving to Iowa, it seemed nothing ever worked for him.

He stopped in front of his desk. It wasn't just his own problems. What was happening to Mom and Dad? They'd had arguments, but Brian had hardly ever heard them scream at each other before. When he first came home and Dad came in to the kitchen, he could have sworn there were tears in his eyes.

It wasn't supposed to be like this. For months before they moved, Dad had told him how cool things would be in Riverside, how Brian would make tons of new friends here in Iowa and Plastisteel would make them so much money. He remembered Dad dreaming about a big house and even a new plane, maybe a twin-engine. Dad used to talk like that for hours, with the same big business smile Alex used when he was suckering someone into a bet.

Just the same as Alex.

Brian sat down at his desk. Alex and Dad were a lot alike. They acted like they had it all figured out, with their cool jokes and answers and advice for everything. But they were just making it up as they went along. Faking it. They were both as clueless as Brian was.

Was that bad? Was that like lying? He closed his eyes and thought about sitting with Wendy on the Runaway Bridge. He could almost feel her hand in his again. And he couldn't be sure, but it really seemed like she wanted to kiss him. He knew he'd wanted to kiss her.

Through the whole wonderful afternoon, Brian hadn't had a clue about what to do. Alex's so-called expert advice had been useless. Everything went well with Wendy when Brian had just stopped worrying so much and guessed what to do, when he took a risk. He too had been making it up as he went along. That had been enough.

Maybe everybody was making it up.

And if that was true, then Brian was just as equipped to handle life as anyone else was, or at least as much as anyone at school.

He opened his eyes and started pacing again. Frankie! He had wanted to pound the guy on the slope. Toss that big dumb jerk into the water and see how he liked it. But when

Brian tried, the guy was just too strong. He'd never beat Frankie physically. Worse, fighting him would upset Wendy.

He went back to his desk and picked up his model SR-71 Blackbird. Grandpa wanted Brian to fight. Wendy didn't. Dad needed Mrs. Douglas to invest in his company, and Mrs. Douglas wouldn't do that until she saw the Plastisteel *Blackbird* fly. Brian brought the model plane in for a landing on his desk. There must be something he could do about all these problems.

Hours later, Brian was lying on his bed with his hands folded behind his head. He wished he could sleep, but too much about the day bothered him. He closed his eyes and tried to get comfortable, but his sore body wouldn't cooperate. The view of the stars out the window was better than any he could have hoped for back in brightly lit Seattle. He watched the stars now and wished they would say something, wished they would tell him what to do.

There was a short hiss of static. "Blackbird, *this is Ground Control. Blackbird, this is Ground Control. Do you copy? Over.*"

The radio! Brian grabbed the handset and pressed the little black button on the side. "Uh, I guess . . . this is *Blackbird.* Max, is that you?"

"*Negative, negative. Code names only on this channel.*"

Also, you must say 'over' when you're done talking. How copy? Over."

Brian laughed. If Max wanted to do the radio all military-style, that was fine. Whatever worked for him. "Ground Control, this is *Blackbird*. Roger. That's a good copy. Over."

"*Blackbird, Ground Control. Hey, I wanted to thank you for trying to help me by the river tonight. I'm sorry you got all dirty because of me. Over."*

Brian waited for a moment, trying to figure out how to answer.

"*Blackbird, this is Ground Control. Did you copy that last transmission? Over."*

He pressed the handset to his face and let out a deep breath. "Ground Control, this is *Blackbird*. Roger. That's a good copy. But I'm the guy who should apologize to you. For a lot of stuff. And . . . starting tomorrow, things are going to be different." Max didn't answer for a while. Then Brian remembered. He keyed the mic again. "Oh. Sorry. Um . . . Over."

"*Thanks, Brian. I really appreciate that. I'd say these radios work great. I'll talk to you tomorrow. Ground Control, out."*

Brian switched off his radio and went to the window to stare at the stars again. A lot had gone wrong since he started school here in Iowa. He was tired of it. Tomorrow, he would start to make some changes.

The next morning, Brian met Wendy skating to school. "Brian, I am so sorry about yesterday," she said.

"Yesterday was great," he said. "I had a lot of fun."

"Yeah, but I mean about my brother —"

"Wendy, it's fine. Really. Don't worry about it."

"It's not fine! I want —"

"Wendy, I'm asking you this as a favor. Please, don't worry about it. Let's just have fun skating! I dare you to keep up!" Brian kicked the pavement to speed up as they hit the Lincoln Street hill. Wendy sped after him. Their race to school ended with a tie and laughter.

The rest of the morning passed normally. Brian didn't know if what he was about to do was right, and he certainly didn't know if it would work or not. He'd have to go for it and hope for the best. Like Alex always did. Like Dad.

As everyone filed out for lunch, Brian approached Ms. Gilbert's desk. She kept reading for a while as he stood there.

Finally, she put a bookmark in and closed the cover. "Yes, Brian? What is it this time?" She thumped the book down on her desk a little hard.

Brian swallowed. "I'm sorry for taking up so much of your reading time at lunch. And also . . ." He thought he better continue before he lost his courage. "Thanks for answering all my questions and everything, but I don't think I'll be staying in here at the start of lunchtime anymore." Ms. Gilbert was still quiet. It was beyond weird. "So, um . . . thank you again. I'm going to go to lunch now."

"Brian?" she said just as he reached the door. "I'm glad you've worked this out. Enjoy your lunch. Welcome to Riverside."

For the first time, Ms. Gilbert actually smiled.

Brian was last in the lunch line again. His mouth watered when the lunch lady put a hot crispito on his tray. Then he went toward the full, loud lunchroom. Alex sat at his table with all the cool guys and Frankie. There wasn't enough room for him. Today, though, that was just what Brian had hoped for.

Max sat by himself two tables away from Alex and the others. He actually unfolded a paper napkin and put it in his lap like he was at some fancy restaurant. Brian made his way to his table and stood waiting while Max had his head bowed in prayer. When he looked up, Brian motioned toward the bench. "Can I sit here?"

He felt awkward, but not due to the people watching and whispering or the giggles from the Wolf Pack. It was awkward to ask to sit with Max because he had been such a jerk to him for so long, while Max had always been a great friend. Brian wanted to start to pay that friendship back.

Max looked surprised, but happy. "Sure. Have a seat. This is a welcome change. I usually eat alone."

"Me too." Brian sat down. "I'm done with that now."

"Hey, Brian!" Frankie shouted. Brian ignored him and took a bite of his delicious crispito. The crunch of the tortilla and the warm meaty goodness in the center tasted like a reward for finally working up the guts to sit with Max in the cafeteria.

"Hey, Roberts. I'm talking to you, new boy."

"Yep, Frankie. I'm new," Brian called back. "Is that really the best you can do? Is that the only way you can insult me, by pointing out the fact that I'm new?"

"No . . . I mean yes. Whatever! Why are you sitting with Mad Max?" Frankie shouted even louder.

"I can sit where I want." Brian tried the peas. They were disgustingly overcooked, merged together into a green paste on the tray. It tasted terrible, but he was happy, knowing Frankie was getting more and more angry as he ate.

"I'm talking to you! Don't think you can ignore me!"

Frankie was so loud now that other kids in the lunchroom were telling him to keep it down. Finally, Mrs.

Valentine walked over to his table. She was young and usually cool, unless someone made her angry. "Frankie, if you can't be quiet you'll be eating in the principal's office for a week!"

Brian caught Max's gaze. They both laughed.

Brian stood at his locker at the end of the day, pulling out *Spitfire* and his backpack. The crowd moved all around him, eager to get out of school. Too many times, he had hidden away from all this, stalling in the classroom, sneaking out the back way, or rushing as fast as he could to be the first one out. Today it felt good to be right in the middle of it all, a part of it.

Max approached. "Would you like to go to the Eagle's Nest?"

Brian checked to make sure nobody could hear them. "I thought *Blackbird* needed more engine parts."

"Yes, but we could research other possible ways to improve engine power."

"I'm not sure I'd be much help with that, but —"

"We could also finish up our mythology assignment," Max said. "Plus, I know of your fondness for cheese puffs. I could bring a bag."

"I'd like to go to the Eagle's Nest," Brian said. "But I'm grounded. I have to go home."

Max's shoulders fell. "Oh. Well, that's okay. I shouldn't have —"

"But my parents never said I couldn't have people over. Just come to my house."

"Really?" Max's face lit up.

"Sure, man."

"Hey, guys," Wendy appeared out of the crowd. Brian immediately checked the hall for Frankie. "Don't worry," she said. "He's outside."

"I wasn't even thinking about him," Brian said.

"Liar." She smiled.

"Hello, Wendy," said Max.

Wendy nodded kindly to Max, then turned to Brian. "Want to thrash tonight?"

Max raised an eyebrow and grinned at Brian before he quietly slipped away.

"I want to," Brian said. After yesterday afternoon with Wendy, there was nothing he'd rather do. "But I'm grounded for coming home all muddy last night."

Wendy looked disappointed. "I'm so sorry. I wish my dad would ground my brother. Frankie needs it." Then she added so quietly that Brian could hardly hear her, "I wish Dad would just do something. Anything."

He reached out and patted her arm. It was a stupid thing to do, maybe. The Wolf Pack would be going crazy about it if they were around. But he didn't think about it when he did it, and now he didn't care. "So anyway, I can't skate with you tonight, but could I walk you part of the way home?"

"Sure," she said.

He slung his backpack over one shoulder and walked out of the school by Wendy's side, switching *Spitfire* to his left just in case she wanted to hold hands again. But before they were even six paces outside the school, he saw a group of guys standing out in the grass. They had formed a circle around Frankie and Max, and Frankie had just knocked Max's books out of his hands.

"Oh, you have to be kidding me," Brian said quietly.

"Brian, please don't —"

"I can't just let him keep picking on me and my friends." He sprinted off toward the crowd.

Frankie slammed his hands into Max's chest. "You're such a loser, Mad Max. With your dorky *Star Trek* books and those idiot glasses." He pushed him again. David, Red, and some of the fourth and fifth grade boys laughed. Alex was watching too. He didn't cheer Frankie on like the other guys did, but he didn't do anything to stop it either.

Brian elbowed his way through the group, knocking David to the side. Alex spotted him and moved to the back of the crowd.

Frankie slapped Max in the head and knocked his glasses off. "Maybe you can have your *Star Trek* ship beam you up, dork."

"Leave him alone, Frankie." Brian stepped into the middle of the circle. He clenched his fists.

Frankie moved closer. That scary twitch was back in his eye. "What's it to you?"

"Max is my friend." He was in it this far. He might as well keep going. "And there's nothing wrong with *Star Trek*! I even have *The Next Generation* Season Four DVD set."

Max had picked up his glasses and was putting them back on. "That's a good one," he said quietly. "The episode 'The Best of Both Worlds' with the Borg and everything. Captain Picard —"

"Max," Brian said. "Later."

Wendy pushed through to join them. "Guys, knock it off. This is stupid."

Frankie held his hands up. "Looks like I'm going to have to beat you both down again."

Great success through great risk. Brian's heart pounded, and he was shaking all over. Now was the time. "No, Frankie. You're done. You leave me and my friends alone. This is your last chance."

Frankie looked at the other guys with an expression that seemed to say, *Can you believe this guy?* Then he stood up straight and flexed his muscles. "What are you gonna do? You want to fight right here? I'll break your face."

Brian didn't flinch. "You just want to fight here in front of the school so some teacher will run to your rescue." He took a step forward, hoping he looked tough. "No. When I beat you, I'm going to beat you completely."

"Nobody is beating anybody, you guys! Just stop it!" Wendy said.

Nobody else said anything. Nobody even seemed to move. They were like vultures, waiting to see who would fall.

"Okay, freak! Right here!" Frankie took a swing but Brian ducked and jumped back. He was so scared that he wanted to throw up, but he also had an idea.

"If you're so sure you can beat me up," he said, "then you can do it just as easily tomorrow down at the skate park." He forced himself to keep his glare fixed on Frankie. "That way no teachers can stop me from finishing you."

Frankie's shoulders heaved up and down as he made a big show of loud breathing through his nose. His eye twitched.

"What's it going to be, tough guy?" Brian said. Then he spoke loudly so everyone could hear. "I tell you what. I'll be at the skate park tomorrow at four thirty, waiting to humiliate you. If you don't show up, everyone will know you're a pathetic coward. It's your choice."

Brian turned away. He paused for a moment when he saw the tears in Wendy's eyes. "I'm sorry," he said. Then he grabbed Max by the arm and pulled him over to Alex. "Eagle's Nest. Right away," he said before leaving the silent crowd, trying not to think about the hurt look on Wendy's face.

The phone was ringing when he made it home. "Hello?" he said, trying to control his breathing so he didn't seem like he had just run into the house.

"Brian, are you okay? You sound out of breath," Mom said.

So much for sounding normal. "I was just . . . um . . . upstairs doing my homework, and I couldn't find the phone."

"Oh," Mom paused for a long time. Did she think he was lying? "Well, just stay in and work. I should get there about six."

"Sure," Brian said. "I have a lot to do anyway. This whole story about Icarus trying to fly."

Mom wished him luck, said good-bye, and hung up. As soon as he was off the phone, Brian grabbed *Spitfire* and set out for the Eagle's Nest as fast as he could.

When he came up out of the tunnel, he found Max and Alex sitting at the table behind *Blackbird*. They just sipped Mountain Dews and stared at him.

"What?" Brian said.

Alex put his can down with a thud. "Dude, what was that all about?"

Max nodded. "I'm grateful for your help, Brian, but I think it is possible you might have an even bigger problem now."

"Possible?" Alex said. "Frankie is going to crush you if you show up to the park tomorrow."

"Whoa, I never said I would fight him," Brian said.

"You said you were going to finish him. Humiliate him. How are you going to do that? It's not like he's just going to stand there and let you —"

"He's not going to be able to do anything." Brian reached into the box and pulled out a Mountain Dew. He popped the top and took a drink. "Boys, let's prep *Blackbird*. She flies tomorrow."

"What are you talking about?" Alex said.

Max frowned. "Brian, I do not believe *Blackbird* is ready. It doesn't have enough power to take off on its own."

"She may have a little trouble taking off, but I've been thinking about our first flight attempt that night, and I bet moving the seats back a bit might shift the weight to put us at a better angle for takeoff. It's a good design, Max. Once she's airborne, she'll fly great."

"But what does *Blackbird* have to do with Frankie Heller?" Alex said.

"Relax," Brian said. "I have a plan."

"Your Mr. Piggly plan nearly got us killed," Alex pointed out.

"I suppose it wouldn't be too difficult to install seat belts," Max said.

Alex ignored Max. "How do you know this idea will work?"

That was a good question. "I don't." Brian shrugged. "But we're going to take our best shot."

Everyone went silent as soon as Brian walked into home-room the next day. Abbie, Heather, and Jess shot him murderous glares. Wendy wouldn't even look at him. B.A., Red, and Dakota all backed out of his way as he went to his desk and sat down.

"I stayed late making the final arrangements," Max said quietly from the seat behind him.

"Don't call them final arrangements, Max. You're not preparing for a funeral," Brian whispered.

Max nodded. "We should be go to throttle up for tonight's mission."

Brian gave him a high five. "Warp speed, Max."

"Hey, Alex, put me down for five bucks," Travis said. "Five on Frankie." He shrugged. "Sorry, Brian."

"I'm sorry too," Brian said. "Sorry you're going to be out five bucks!"

"Okay," Alex said. "I have Travis in for five dollars on Frankie in this evening's confrontation. Loser is whoever leaves the park first, right?"

"Yeah, if the loser can even get up to run away," said Red. "Once I was on vacation with my family at this campground in Oklahoma, and there was this big cowboy guy from Texas with boots, hat, spurs, the whole thing. Anyway, this cowboy guy kept bugging my cousin. So I told him if he didn't leave her alone, I'd have to fight him. The cowboy just says, 'Don't mess with Texas.' So I punched him." He brought his fist up. "Bam! Uppercut! I hit him so hard the guy actually came off his feet up in the air. He fell back and hit the ground. Out cold." Red shook his head. "I'm just real lucky he didn't die."

B.A. burst out laughing. "Red said!"

"Red said!" Travis yelled. The rest of the guys joined in.

"I'm serious!" Red shouted. "It's true. You can ask my cousin!"

B.A. waved them all quiet. "I watched Brian beat Frankie in the toughest eating contest I've ever seen. I bet five on Brian."

Alex typed the bet into his iPhone. "B.A. bets five bucks that Brian will still be in the park after Frankie has left tonight. Is that right?"

"Yep!" B.A. nodded. "I'm with you."

"Thanks," Brian said.

Alex grinned at Brian. "Dude, we're going to make so much money on this with just my commission alone. Everybody thinks Frankie's going to crush your skull in! Between that and the bets on tonight's football game . . ." He laughed like an evil genius. "I'm seeing green!"

"That's good, I guess," Brian said. "You're keeping it clear, right? It's about the last one remaining in the park."

"Brian," Max said. "Alex knows gambling. He'll take care of it."

It was the best morning Brian could remember in Iowa.

At lunch that afternoon, Brian sat with Max. He was getting more and more nervous about that afternoon, but still forced himself to try to eat his piece of pizza.

"Can I sit with you guys?" Alex said as he approached with his tray.

Max made a big show of looking up and down their otherwise empty table. "There does appear to be room."

Brian could hear the whispers as Alex sat down at their most uncool lunch table.

"Whatever!" Frankie said loudly from the popular table. "If he wants to sit with the losers, let him!"

"I know I take up a lot of space, but could you squeeze one more in?" B.A. sat down with two pieces of pizza. "I keep telling my dad that he should put pizza on the menu at Piggly's, but he never does."

"I need a change of pace," Red said as he took a seat. "Figure I'll sit here today."

Brian had to chuckle a little when he saw the big grin on Max's face. "I should have done this a long time ago," he said quietly.

The last bell of the school day finally rang. Action time. Alex pulled his phone out of his pocket and handed it to Brian. "You guys ready?"

Brian nodded. "Let's go for it."

"Agreed. Timing is critical. Gentlemen . . ." said Max, "begin Phase One."

They had worked out the plan last night in the Eagle's Nest. First, Brian had to get home to take the three-thirty call from his parents. He skated like a madman and made it into the house with a few minutes to spare, switching on the PRC-77 radio as soon as he was inside.

Brian was supposed to take Mom's call at three thirty and then start Phase Two immediately, but it was three forty before the phone rang. He answered right away. "Hello."

"Oh. Brian. I don't think the phone even had time to ring," Mom said. "How was school?"

"Fine," Brian said.

"Anything interesting happen?"

"Nope."

"Blackbird, *this is Ground Control. Radio check. Over.*" Max's voice squawked loud on the radio. Brian had the volume up way too high. He turned it down.

"What was that?" Mom asked. "Do you have boys over? You're grounded, remember? You need to tell them to —"

"No, Mom. It's just the radio. The music radio, I mean."

"What other kind —"

"I put it on because it helps me study. I have so much homework. I should really go, or I'll be up all night, trying to get all of this homework done."

"Blackbird, *where are you? Answer the radio! Over!*" It was Alex this time.

"What do you have for homework tonight?" Mom asked.

Was she kidding? She hadn't asked about his homework this whole school year and she picked today to start? "I have to read . . . um . . . an article about . . . the . . . um . . . guys who flew the first airplane."

"The Wright Brothers."

"Yep. Those guys."

"Well, that will be great. You love airplanes."

"Sure do. It's a really long article, though, so I better go." Brian paced the dining room. He wanted to scream. They were so behind schedule.

"Well, okay. I'm sorry, but we'll probably be a little late getting home tonight. So much work to do. I promise that it'll let up soon and it won't be like this always."

"Sure, I understand. I really should go, though."

"Okay. Enjoy your afternoon. I love you."

"Sure love you too bye." Brian hung up the phone and grabbed the handset on the PRC-77. He pressed the little black rubber button. "Ground Control, this is *Blackbird*. I read you loud and clear. Over."

Almost immediately static popped and Max was back on the radio. "Blackbird, *this is Ground Control. We are behind schedule! What's your status? Over.*"

Brian radioed back. "Ground Control, *Blackbird*. Mom's call came late. I'm going to call Grandpa right now. I'll leave the mic keyed so you can hear what I say. When I say, 'It's good to talk to you,' then begin Phase Two. Over."

"*Roger that,* Blackbird. *Ground Control is standing by. Over.*"

Brian grabbed Alex's cell phone and dialed Grandpa's number. Grandpa had a really old-fashioned phone with a curly rubber cord. When the phone rang, he'd have to go to the living room or his bedroom to answer it. He wouldn't be able to look out his kitchen window and see the guys bringing *Blackbird* out of the Eagle's Nest in broad daylight.

"Hello?" Grandpa's voice sounded tired.

"Hi, Grandpa. Do you have a second?" Brian said. He was still holding down the TRANSMIT button on the radio handset, and he brought it over close to the cell phone. "It's good to talk to you." He let go of the button. The guys would know they could make their move.

"It's good to talk to you too." Grandpa yawned. "I'm glad you called. I was taking a little nap and slept too late. Probably won't be able to sleep tonight." Brian put the PRC-77 radio into his backpack, slipped into the shoulder straps, and headed out the door with *Spitfire*, the cell phone still at his ear. Grandpa coughed. "So what's on your mind?"

"Well, I have this school project." Brian planned to tell him about an assignment he'd researched online. "I have to interview a family member to ask when our family first came to America. Then I have to write a report about it." He dropped his skateboard on the street and started up the Fourth Street slope to Lincoln.

"Really, now. Well, this is actually a good story. You see, my grandmother came to this country from Germany with her parents and her older brother in, ooh, the late 1800s or early 1900s. I'll have to look it up. I have her obituary in a box somewhere. She used to tell me this story when I was a boy. Now, they had to cross the Atlantic by ship. Not so many planes in those days."

Brian listened while Grandpa kept talking. No way was he going to leave that phone and see the guys moving *Blackbird*. At Lincoln Street, he hooked a left to catch up with Alex and Max, who would be taking the flyer around the back of the big hill on which Riverside was built. They had agreed it would be hard to carry *Blackbird* through the north woods, but better that than to be spotted before takeoff.

"All the immigrants at Ellis Island had to be checked to make sure they weren't bringing in any diseases," Grandpa said. "Well, my grandmother's mother wiped her eye. Nothing special. Just the way people sometimes wipe their eyes. But an immigration officer spotted this and pulled her mother into a separate room. Her father sat her and her brother down and told them, in German of course, 'If they will not let your mother in, we will all have to go back.'"

"*Blackbird, this is Ground Control. We're clear of the Eagle's Nest. We could use your help carrying the package. Over.*"

Now Brian had to find a way to end this phone call with Grandpa. "We will . . . all . . . have . . . to go . . . back." He spoke very slowly as if he were saying it out loud while he wrote it down. "But they got in. That's great. That's the perfect story. Thanks, Grandpa!"

"But there's more. They came to Iowa and settled on a farm —"

"Right. Got it. I better go work on this paper. It has to be typed and everything. Can I call you back if I have more questions?"

"Sure. Anytime."

"Thanks, Grandpa. Bye." Brian ended the call and slipped the phone in his pocket as he rolled to the end of Lincoln Street, where the pavement ended and a gravel road headed out to the country.

"Dude, hurry up!" Alex's shout came from the woods off to the right. Brian tied *Spitfire* to his backpack and ran across the field to join the guys and *Blackbird*. Max waved at him. Alex, carrying the other radio in his own backpack, along with a small black bag slung from his shoulder, nodded toward the empty corner of the flyer. "We have to hurry. If Frankie gets to the park and you're too late, he'll say you were too chicken to show up. Then I'll lose a bunch of money."

"You bet on me?" Brian asked. They rotated the flyer to get it around a bush.

"I bet on *Blackbird* taking off," said Alex. "It's a long shot, but sometimes you just have to go for it."

They came out of the trees beside Riverside Road.

"We should cross quickly, before a car comes along and we are discovered," said Max.

They scurried across the open road as fast as they could. "Good thing she's so light," Brian said.

"Actually, it is slightly lighter than usual," Max said. "The fuel tank is empty. I hid a gas can with my bicycle, the rope, and the weapon at the takeoff point."

Finally, they came to the edge of the woods near the dead end at the top of the Seventh Street hill. They carried the aircraft through the weeds up to the edge of the road. Ahead and off to the right was a big white house.

"It is perhaps a great irony that the biggest hill in town has Frankie Heller's house right on top of it," said Max.

They put *Blackbird* down in the tall grass next to Max's bike and ducked down to hide. They had a perfect view of the house. If Frankie was already waiting at the park, they could just take off in time to meet him. If he hadn't left yet, they would know when he did.

Max put a plastic funnel into the spout on the fuel tank and then filled it up from the gas can. Alex took Brian's radio and slipped it into the wire basket they'd added to the back of the pilot's seat. He put the other radio in the dorky-looking basket on the front of Max's bike. Brian tied a rope to the special hook they'd installed under the engine's support beam, and tied the other end to Max's backseat handlebars. Then he checked the tightness of the clamps on the NX-03, the new silver rocket Max had installed on his bike.

Alex slipped the camera out of its carrying bag and gently handed it to Max. "This is my dad's. It's the most expensive thing ever. You need to get a lot of good video of the flight, but whatever happens, don't mess up the camera."

They sat in silence for a while. Max took off his glasses and wiped them on his shirt. Then he chewed the earpiece. "I don't know about this, Brian. Maybe we should abort the mission."

"This is going to work, Max! I've thought about this a lot, and you can't wait around for a situation to get better. You make a choice. You have to *take* that risk for greatness." He took a deep breath. "At the skate park before the first day of school, Wendy asked if I could *get* air. But flying doesn't come naturally." He pointed at Max. "You have to be smart." He nodded at Alex. "You have to take the big gamble." He held his fist up. "You have to *steal* air."

Just then, Frankie came out his front door and walked away from them, heading toward the park. They waited a while to let him get ahead.

"Begin Phase Three," Brian said. "Let's do this."

A few minutes later, *Blackbird* was in position in the middle of Seventh Street at the top of the hill. Max rolled his bike about fifteen feet down the street, until the rope they'd strung between the flyer and the bike was taut. Then he walked back.

"I think we're ready to begin. Gentlemen, please take your seats." Brian and Alex sat down in the pilot and copilot chairs. Max nodded to Brian. "You are familiar with the controls." He pointed at a red lever that had been installed to the left of the yoke. "This is new. Pulling that disengages the tow rope."

"Good to know," said Brian.

Max walked around toward the back of the aircraft. "Alex, once again, you'll be in charge of the brakes. Remember, it's important that you push both levers down at the same time and keep them pushed down until they lock." He returned to Brian's side and looked down the street. "I'm still not entirely confident about this."

Brian gave him a light punch to the shoulder. "Max, you said *Blackbird* doesn't have enough power to get up to take-off speed on a level runway. So, we start the engine and throttle her up, you pull us with the rocketbike, and we're all rolling down the steepest hill in Riverside. With that much speed, *Blackbird* will take off just fine."

"Come on! We have to hurry! Time is literally money here, guys!" Alex said.

Max ran back to the weeds and returned with two damp cloth sacks. "I almost forgot our weapon."

Alex wrinkled his nose and waved his hand in front of his face. "Unh, that smells worse than it did yesterday."

"Good," said Brian. "They'll work even better, then."

"But why this?" Alex said. "Why not a basket of eggs or something? We could have mounted a slingshot and shot the eggs one at a time."

"Eggs cost money." Max shrugged. "This was free."

Alex grabbed the tops of the bags and rested the bottoms on the back corners of both skateboards. "Still, we didn't have to get the soupiest stuff."

"Let's go!" Brian shouted.

"Good luck," Max said.

"We'll need it," said Alex.

Max ran ahead and got on his bike. He gave the thumbs-up. Brian grabbed the handle for the starter cord and yanked hard. The engine sputtered a little. "Come on, *Blackbird*," he said. "I need you, girl." He pulled the cable again. The propeller spun to life with a roar. Either *Blackbird* would fly, or they'd roll down the hill and crash. There was no backing out now.

Max hit a button on the NX-03 and then started to pedal. Fire burst out of the end of the rocket and the bike shot forward. The rope went tight and *Blackbird* jerked so hard that Brian was pressed to the back of his chair.

"Oh yeah!" Alex shouted over the noise of the engine, the rocket, and the wind.

They rolled faster and faster down the hill, crossing Lincoln Street in moments. Brian pushed the throttle up to give the engine more power and pulled the yoke toward him. When they cleared Tilford Street, *Blackbird* rose from the ground about two feet.

"We're flying!" Alex said.

But something was wrong. The flyer crashed back down to the ground and rolled some more. It felt like their speed had leveled out. *Blackbird* did another quick jump and then hit the ground.

"Not again!" Alex yelled.

No. Not again. Everything was riding on this flight: saving the company, beating Frankie — everything. They had to fly now. Brian shouted to Alex, "We gotta lose some weight! We're too heavy for takeoff. Drop one of the sacks!"

"I can't!" Alex yelled back. "*Blackbird* is balanced. If I dump one sack, we might tip over."

"Then drop one bag and center the other!"

"It's cow poop, dude! These bags are soaked through with it!"

"Alex, drop a bag! Do it now, or we're not going to make it!"

Alex screamed as he pushed one sack of manure soup onto the street and pulled the other into his lap. "Aw man, you owe me a new pair of pants!"

Brian squinted his eyes and gritted his teeth. "Come on, baby. Come on, baby," he whispered. He held the yoke in one hand and patted the wing with the other. "Now, girl!" *Blackbird* rose up two feet. Then three. Four feet. She kept rising, speeding up.

"The tow rope!" Alex shouted.

"Oh crap!" Brian had almost forgot. He yanked the red lever. The rope fell away. Seven feet. Eight. They soared up into the sky. Brian could feel himself pushed down into his seat.

"Warp speed!" he shouted.

Power lines crossed the road ahead. Brian slammed the yoke forward and the flyer dove down under them, but he still ducked. When they were clear of the cables, he pulled up, bringing *Blackbird* a hundred feet above the trees. He worked the foot pedals to operate the tail rudder and pushed the yoke to the right, banking to starboard. In a moment they flew over Carl Jacobs Park in the middle of the square downtown. He leveled the wings and steered just with the rudder.

They were flying. Really flying. All the hard work had paid off. *Blackbird* was airborne.

"Wooooooo!" Brian shouted. "This is awesome!"

"We're flying! We are flying!" Alex laughed. "This is so fun, I almost don't even care that a sack of manure's in my lap. We're really, really flying!"

Grandpa's farm was ahead to the right. The giant barn appeared small from up here. Brian thought back to when he and Alex had first swung from the rope in the hayloft, wondering what it would be like to be higher. Now they knew. He pulled back and right on the yoke and *Blackbird* soared up and to the north.

"Brian," Alex shouted. "Max is on the radio. He says something like the NX-03 rocket was a success."

"That just means the rocket burned out safely," Brian called back. "His first two rockets exploded after ignition."

They were flying high now over the north woods. Brian laughed out loud. "This is the greatest! Let's get crazy!" He pushed the yoke forward and to the right, diving and banking tightly. The trees below seemed to grow as *Blackbird* dropped closer to them.

"Um, Brian?" Alex said.

"I've got it." He straightened their roll and pulled the yoke to bring *Blackbird* out of her dive. There was a little bump. "What was that?"

"Dude, the back wheels just clipped the top of that tree!"

"Whoops." Brian wiped his forehead and brought *Blackbird* over Riverside, heading south toward the river. He banked out in a wide curve to get a little room and then came in line with the river, about two hundred feet up. The giant white cement towers of the grain elevators were dead ahead.

"What are you doing?" Alex asked.

"She's not a commercial jet. We built her to fly. Let's really *fly*!" They drew closer and closer to the grain elevators. Brian centered *Blackbird* on the space between two of the towers, a gap of maybe six feet.

"Brian, look out!"

At the last moment he cranked the yoke to port, dipping the left wing down sharply and the right nearly straight up. There was a rush of displaced air as they shot through the small space, and a quick jerk of the yoke righted the wings. He pulled up. The American flag fluttered in the breeze on top of the towers behind them. "Yeah!"

"I'm so glad we put in seat belts," Alex said.

Brian kept their raised pitch, letting *Blackbird* gain altitude while steering to the south. Soon they were even higher than they'd been with Mr. Piggly.

"Ground Control, this is *Blackbird*." Alex must have been yelling into the radio. "That's a good copy. Over."

"What's up?" Brian said.

"Max says he's at the park. The target is in position, and we should begin Phase Four."

"Roger that," Brian said. He reversed course to fly back north to Riverside. "Let's see what *Blackbird* can do! I'm going to drop altitude again, and we'll do a flyby pass of the park to see where Frankie is. Then we'll bring her around for our attack run."

"Yeah!" Alex shouted. "Come on, *Blackbird*! You can do it!"

He'd been waiting for this moment. Brian pushed forward on the yoke. He felt his body lighten in his seat a little as the aircraft headed down. There was no way to gauge their speed, but it sure felt like they were flying faster. He worked the foot pedals to adjust the tail rudder and keep them in line with the park. They were up maybe three hundred feet.

In a few minutes, they were close enough for Brian to turn to port. Down below, little dots of people had gathered near the skate ramps in Riverview Park. Brian slammed the yoke forward and *Blackbird* dove at a steep angle. Alex let out a whoop behind him, but Brian focused on the maneuver. He could feel the aircraft shaking. The park and the kids in it appeared to grow larger. Some of them were shouting and pointing up at *Blackbird*.

Frankie had his hand up, keeping the sun out of his eyes to get a better look at the approaching aircraft. "There you are," Brian said quietly to himself. Frankie started moving off toward home.

"He's trying to get away!" Alex yelled.

"Not a chance!" Brian banked the flyer and shot down again to cut him off. They swooped by only about four feet from the ground, close to a dozen feet in front of Frankie.

People, trees, ramps passed by in a blur. Brian pulled up, soaring back into the air. They were past the park already. He used the river as a ground guide to maneuver to port and get lined up with the park again.

"Let's do it!" Brian yelled.

"Ground Control, this is *Blackbird*," Alex said. "We are in position now. We're starting our approach for the attack run. Over!" There was a pause. "Roger that, Ground Control. That's a good copy. Talk to you after it's over. *Blackbird* out!"

"You ready, Alex?" Brian asked. Riverview Park was coming into range again. He eased the flyer down to maybe two hundred feet.

"Max says he's worked out the geometry," Alex yelled. "We need to pass about three feet above Frankie's head, then it's bombs away when we're eight feet in front of him. Whoa!"

Brian pushed the yoke forward and *Blackbird* plummeted toward the ground. They picked up speed as they descended, moving so fast that the flyer shook again. All the kids were watching them. Some clapped. Some pointed. Frankie moved a little to the right. Brian adjusted course to keep him centered.

"Brian, are you sure she'll pull out of this?"

"Get ready, Alex!" They had seconds until they were in range. One poop bomb, one shot. He brought *Blackbird* out of her dive so they'd just barely pass above Frankie. Thirty feet. Fifteen. Eight. "Now! Now! Now!"

"Bomb away!" Alex shouted.

Brian pulled back on the yoke to bring *Blackbird* back up, but he didn't even watch where they were flying. Instead, he looked back to see the blob of thick wet manure expand. The soupy dark brown poop slammed into Frankie so hard that he went flying back off his feet. He flailed his arms, landing on his butt.

"We nailed him!" Brian yelled. He put *Blackbird* in a tight low curve. "Alex, you timed it perfectly!"

"Dude, it plastered him!" Alex laughed, but then stopped. "Ground Control, this is *Blackbird*, go ahead. Over."

Brian brought them around toward the Runaway Bridge and did a dive run under it. He pulled up to gain altitude.

"Max says everyone is cracking up," Alex said. "Frankie is spitting manure out of his mouth and wiping it from his eyes and nose. He's not sure, but he thinks Frankie might be crying."

"Let's go check it out," Brian said. They'd turned around and were coming up on the park again. He brought it in at a low twenty feet. Frankie saw them and started running out of the park toward home. "There he goes!" Brian laughed. "But we're still here. Looks like you won your bet."

"I always win!" Alex said.

Down below, their classmates clapped, laughed, and cheered. Brian dipped a wing to them and then took *Blackbird* up high. They'd done it.

"Brian, Max says he has no idea how fast *Blackbird* burns fuel, so we shouldn't take any chances. We should go ahead with Phase Five and bring it in for a landing heading north on First Street. It's at the bottom of the hill and should be level enough."

"Roger that," Brian said. He put *Blackbird* through a series of maneuvers that lined them up with First Street.

"Watch for cars and power lines," Alex said.

They were coming in nice and shallow, maybe twenty or twenty-five feet up, just like Dad bringing the Cardinal in for a landing on some little grass airstrip. Brian eased the throttle lever forward and felt the engine power down a little. The flyer began to descend. "Be ready on those brakes," he shouted to Alex, but he did not look away from the street. Twenty feet. Ten. Five feet up. They were just above the pavement. He eased the yoke forward and throttled all the way down. The skateboards made smooth contact. Brian hit the kill switch to shut the engine off. "Brake! Brake! Brake!"

"I can't . . . stupid things . . ." Alex muttered. A horrible screeching noise came from the rear of the aircraft.

Brian felt them slow down a little, but there wasn't much more he could do. He lowered the horizontal stabilizer to push the nose down a little, but given that they were rolling on two skateboards, they could pretty much move only in a straight line.

They had maybe two blocks to go until First Street intersected with Lincoln Street. The yellow house directly ahead loomed closer and closer. "Why aren't we stopping?" Brian turned around. Two trails of thick black smoke rose from the ground below *Blackbird*.

"I got 'em locked down! The door stopper things are just burning up!" Alex said.

One block to go. They were still moving too fast. "Dude, these brakes are useless!" Alex's whole body jerked as he tried to push them down harder, then he jumped back as sparks shot out. "The rubber's all burned off. We're grinding metal!"

"Flintstones brakes!" Brian shouted.

"What are you talking about?"

"Come on! Do it!" He leaned back in his seat and pressed the soles of his shoes to the street.

"Do you know how much these shoes cost?" Alex said.

"Do it now!" Brian's legs shook as his shoes skidded along the pavement. He heard another scraping noise and saw Alex was dragging his feet as well.

"First my pants. Now my shoes. Want to ruin my shirt next?" said Alex.

Blackbird rolled across Lincoln Street and up a slightly sloped driveway. They were eight feet from smashing right through the Iowa Hawkeyes mascot painted on the white garage door. They rolled closer and closer. Brian cringed and instinctively held his hands up in front of him. "Stop, stop, stop, stop!"

Blackbird scraped to a halt about two feet from the garage door.

Brian finally let out a breath. His heart pounded in his chest. He looked back at Alex. "Touchdown."

Alex was shaking. He slowly nodded as he fumbled for the radio handset. When he picked it up, he took a deep breath. "Ground —" He swallowed and licked his lips. "Ground Control, this is *Blackbird*. *Blackbird* has landed. I say again, *Blackbird* has landed. We're at First and Lincoln. How copy? Over." Brian could hear the faint sound of Max's voice on the radio. Alex frowned. "Negative, Ground Control. I just said '*Blackbird* has landed.' I didn't say it was a safe landing. *Blackbird* out." He switched off the radio and clipped the handset to the wire basket. Then he looked at Brian and pointed at Herky the Hawk on the door right in front of them. "Whoa."

Brian nodded. "As Max would say, 'precisely.'"

Brian and Alex stepped down off of *Blackbird* and onto solid ground. They picked the flyer up, each carrying a wing. They intended to hide it in the north woods until dark, when they could safely sneak it back to the Eagle's Nest, but before they could carry it very far, Max rode up on his two-seat bike. Wendy was pedaling in the back.

They put the flyer down as Max ran up to them. "I believe the mission was a resounding success! I'm a little concerned by the trails the brakes seem to have made in the street, but the flying was impressive."

"Yeah, Max, about those brakes . . ." Alex said as he checked the worn bottoms of his shoes.

Brian left the two of them and went over to talk to Wendy. "Hey," he said.

"Hey," said Wendy.

Was she angry? Did she hate him for what he'd done? Maybe she'd come here to say she never wanted to talk to him or to slap him or something. "I um . . . sort of poop-bombed your brother."

"I saw that." Wendy shook her head. "I suppose you had to do something. Frankie needed to be taught a lesson."

"It was the only one we could think of," Brian said.

She laughed quietly. "Really? Poop? That's all you could think of?"

"Sorry."

Wendy reached out and squeezed his hand. His heart beat heavier than it had when they'd nearly crashed into the garage. She smiled at him. "I'm just happy you didn't fight him."

"I thought I'd try something new."

"You . . . kept your promise . . . I guess." She moved closer. He looked into her amazing green eyes, and she looked back at him.

"Hey, you two," Alex said. Brian and Wendy jumped apart. "We need help carrying *Blackbird*. We have to hide it before everyone finds us or we'll never get it put away tonight."

"I gotta go," Brian said to Wendy. He hoped she'd understand.

Wendy stepped away from him and picked up Max's bike. "I'll take this to Max's house. Then I'll call you tonight," she said. "And you don't have to worry about my brother. If Frankie ever manages to get the stink washed off, he'll think twice before bothering you again."

Brian ran to take hold of *Blackbird*. They carried it around the back of the house they'd almost hit, across a grassy field, and deep into the north woods.

"Dude, do you have my dad's camera?" Alex asked once they'd hid the flyer under some thick bushes. Max unslung his backpack and pulled out the device. Alex took it from him and checked it over. "Whew. It looks okay. If it was messed up, I'd be a dead man." He hit a couple buttons. After a minute or two, video came up on the little flip-out screen. "Beautiful." He showed the screen to Brian. "Check it out. In high def too."

The zoom on the camera was impressive. Close-ups showed *Blackbird* in flight with her Plastisteel wings and tail shining in the afternoon sun, and long-distance shots caught the flyer swooping over buildings or dodging around trees. Max had even filmed their crazy banking maneuver between the grain elevators. With a little editing, the video was sure to razzle-dazzle Mrs. Douglas. Max had also scored perfect footage of Frankie getting nailed by the wet manure bomb.

"Awesome," Brian said. "We can send a copy to Frankie, and if he tries to be a tough guy again, we'll just threaten to put the video online."

"Guys, seriously, this was probably the coolest thing I've ever done. This was something real." Alex rubbed his knuckles under his chin. "Magazines, television . . . They're going to pay so much for our story." He laughed a little. "I'm going to start tracking down people who owe me money. B.A. has some winnings coming too."

Knowing they'd be back for *Blackbird* soon, they walked out of the woods and headed home.

At one o'clock the next day, Alex, Brian, and Max were up in Brian's room. "Gentlemen, ties." Alex tossed pre-knotted neckties to the other two. "Brian, you said your shirt was stained." He looked at Brian's dingy dress shirt and handed him a jacket. "I brought this from home. See if it fits."

The jacket's sleeves came up several inches too short when Brian finally wiggled into the thing. He sighed and put his hands on his hips.

"Better than letting everyone see those mud stains," said Alex.

"It *is* an improvement." Max did not sound very convincing.

The sound of a car outside drew Brian to his window for the hundredth time. Earlier, he had watched Max and his parents arrive in their Prius and Grandpa in his pickup. A few minutes after that, Alex and his mom, dad, and sister had pulled up in their Lexus. The latest car rolled right by — not the vehicle he was hoping for.

"Brian," said Max, "no doubt everyone downstairs is wondering why we called this meeting. It was not easy to get my parents to come."

"Yeah," said Alex. "My dad was supposed to drop Mom and Katie off at the mall when he went in to the office. It took some time to convince them this was important."

"We wouldn't even be having this meeting if you hadn't uploaded the video to the Internet," Brian said.

Alex held his hands up. "Dude, what could I do? Someone put up a crappy video he took with his phone. It was starting to get a lot of views. I had to put up our good video to stay on top of publicity. How was I supposed to know it would go viral so fast?"

"In any case, Brian, we can't change what is already done," said Max.

They were right, and they couldn't just leave everyone downstairs wondering what was going on either. "We'll just have to start," Brian said.

"Remember, play it professional." Alex straightened his tie and picked a piece of lint off his blue jacket. He looked like one of those guys at expensive boarding schools that Brian had seen in movies. "They're going to find out about *Blackbird* soon anyway. We might as well tell them ourselves."

"It's the most logical approach," said Max.

Alex rolled his eyes. "Thanks, Spock."

Max frowned. "I consider it a compliment to be compared to the greatest Vulcan who —"

"Oh, come on," Brian said, leading the way out of the room before Max and Alex could get into a *Star Trek* debate. This meeting would be like skating, flying, or almost anything else. It was best to just go for it.

Downstairs in the living room, Brian's and Max's parents sat on chairs brought in from the dining room, while Grandpa sat in the old leather recliner. Mr. and Mrs. Mackenzie occupied either end of the couch, with Alex's little sister Katie pouting in the middle. She perked up when Brian and the guys entered the room, giggling and giving Brian a little wave.

"What's this all about?" Brian's father asked once again. Even with Max and Alex at his side, Brian felt his courage slipping away.

"Yes, I'd like to know too," said Alex's mom. "Alex, if you wanted us to meet your new friends, you could have —"

"I'll handle this," said Mr. Mackenzie. "Alex, you said this was important business and —"

"Can I have your attention please?" Brian spoke loudly. If this was going to work out right, they would have to be the ones to lead the discussion. "We have to tell you something that is probably going to surprise you."

"But it's good!" Alex cut in.

How did Dad know how to run meetings like this? Brian smiled. Dad made it up. "That's right! It is good. So just, please, listen to the whole presentation before you make judgments."

"Oh no," Brian's mom said. "What's wrong?"

Brian shot a questioning look at Max, who shrugged. No help there. Alex was fiddling with his iPhone.

Brian took a deep breath. There was no delicate way to put this. "Max built an airplane, and we flew it."

"You built a toy airplane?" said Alex's dad. "Like radio controlled? There's no way you could have built a real plane." He rubbed his hand over his bald spot.

"Why doesn't anyone ever believe me?" Max whispered.

"*Blackbird* is totally real," Alex said. "Brian and I flew it, flew *on* it, yesterday."

He finished messing with his iPhone and held it up, showing the video of *Blackbird* in action. Everyone went still and quiet as they watched, except for little Katie, who kept smiling at Brian.

As the video ended, the adults all seemed to erupt into conversation at once.

"You could have been hurt flying around on that thing!" Brian's mom said.

Mrs. Mackenzie leaned forward in her seat. "You didn't even wear a helmet?"

"Were you working from a kit or plans you found online?" Dr. Warrender asked.

Max cut in, "Actually, I designed *Blackbird* myself."

Mr. Warrender raised an eyebrow. "The results are remarkable."

"Even if the methods are a bit unorthodox," Dr. Warrender added. Max's parents were the only ones smiling, though his mom looked like she was trying to conceal it. Max made no effort to hide his big grin.

"You were supposed to be grounded, Brian," Mom said. "Am I going to have to send you to your grandfather's house after school to make sure you don't go running off before I get home?"

Brian risked eye contact with Grandpa. The old man seemed very serious, but there was a little gleam in his eye. He only nodded.

Alex's father stood up, still rubbing his bald spot. "You boys will be in junior high next year. It's time for you to start being serious and thinking about your reputations and your futures. This kind of . . . cowboy stuff won't help you."

Brian thought he heard Alex laugh just a little bit. Cowboy stuff? Futures? Fixing the future of Synthtech was what the whole flyer thing was all about. At least, that was how it started. He looked over at Max and Alex. The *Blackbird* project had become a lot more than just a cool experiment or a way to help Dad's company.

Dr. Warrender frowned. "The material of that plane looked rather familiar. What is it made from?"

"Yeah." Brian kept up that business smile until his cheeks hurt. "It's Plastisteel." He held up his hand against the outburst from his dad and Dr. Warrender.

"I'm sorry," said Mrs. Mackenzie. "Plasti-what?"

"It's my invention," said Dr. Warrender. She explained Plastisteel and Synthtech to Alex's family. Alex's dad raised his eyebrows, and his mom looked similarly impressed. Dad's face was bright red as he glared at Brian. Instead of being angry, Brian's mother turned away and wiped tears from her eyes.

"Just wait a second," Brian cut in. Alex elbowed him, and he remembered his manners. "Please." He tried to act casual. "When we borrowed . . . stole the materials for the flyer, we didn't realize how difficult it would be for you all to make more."

"Brian, we needed that Plastisteel," Dr. Warrender said. "Do you have any idea how important it was?"

"As regards the theft," said Max. "I was the one who actually —"

"Who actually was mad at me for stealing —" Brian started, trying to keep Max from taking all the blame.

"We were all in on that part together," Alex said. "We are very sorry."

"Brian, the least you could have done was think about the future of your family's business," Dad said. "If you hadn't stolen the Plastisteel, we might have had some compelling demonstration for Mrs. Douglas or even —"

"That's what I'm trying to tell you," Brian said. "We contacted Mrs. Douglas and showed her video footage of our flight. She was so impressed that she agreed to —"

"What!" Brian's dad yelled. "You had no right to contact my business associate!"

"Oh, relax, Jack!" Mrs. Douglas herself stood in the entryway to the living room. "The door was open. Hope you don't mind that I let myself in."

Brian whispered to Alex, "It's about time she showed up."

Dad clapped his hands together and grinned. "Not at all, Mrs. Douglas. What an unexpected pleasure."

"Not unexpected at all! These fine young gentlemen in their sharp ties invited me."

Brian's dad wiped his forehead. "We were just discussing —"

"I know. I could hear your discussion all the way out in the street." She noticed Alex's dad. "Hello, Josh. How's business?"

"Helen. Great to see you again. Business is . . . um . . . great."

Mrs. Douglas looked unimpressed. "I'll bet."

"How's your car running?" Mr. Mackenzie asked.

"Perfectly, of course. If not, you'd be hearing from me."

"Happy to help!" Mr. Mackenzie said with a big fake grin. "Anything for you."

Was there no end to the kissing up to Mrs. Douglas? Brian wondered.

"Incredible machine," Mrs. Douglas said.

"Well, Lexus builds the best, I always say," said Mr. Mackenzie.

"I'm sure you say that, especially since you sell them," said Mrs. Douglas. "But I was talking about a different incredible machine." She reached into her purse and pulled out an iPad. "Craziest thing. I received this video clip in my e-mail last night." She touched the screen a couple times and showed them the video of *Blackbird* swooping around Riverside. "Ding-dangedest thing I ever saw. Look at her go! Oh, watch this part where she flies right between those towers. Woo!" She smiled. "I love that. Then I laughed and laughed so hard at the part coming up where they poop-bomb some kid in the park. A poop bomb! That's funny!"

She glared at everyone else in the room. Dad laughed first, and then the rest of the adults joined in.

Brian watched Frankie getting splattered on the video. "I thought you were taking that part out," he whispered to Alex. Alex shrugged.

"I saw the video of this amazing aircraft, and I could almost hear my mama talking to me." Mrs. Douglas held up her right hand and looked up. "She said, 'Angel, I know you don't need any more money. You're richer than fling fiddle! But look at that plane fly! Made out of crazy magic plastic. You're over sixty and your fourth husband bores you to tears. Have a little fun. You deserve it!'" She put her hand down and looked at the others. "Don't I deserve it?"

"Absolutely!" Dad said.

"Of course," said Mr. Mackenzie.

"I think so," said Mom.

"That's what I thought," said Mrs. Douglas. "So I decided I'd come down here today and see if there was anything my money and I could do to help you whoop up this magic plastic faster." She tapped her iPad screen a few times and then handed the device to Brian's father. "And we'll have to hurry, because I took the liberty of talking to some friends of mine who work in engineering and manufacturing, and they just might be interested in making some very substantial purchases."

Dad's business smile disappeared when he saw whatever was on the screen. His mouth fell open. "Um . . . Are you serious about these numbers?"

"Sweetheart," Mrs. Douglas said, "with dollar amounts that large, I'm always serious. So why don't you let the kiddies here go play so we can talk real business?"

"Mrs. Douglas," Mom said, "they've done something that requires they be disciplined."

"What?" Mrs. Douglas acted like this was the most outrageous news she'd ever heard. "These perfect little angels in trouble? What? You afraid they're going to get hurt with their little airplane?"

"Where is this airplane now?" Max's dad asked.

"Yes, let's make sure there are no more of these dangerous flights," said Mom.

"We don't have it anymore," Brian said almost without thinking. All eyes were on him. Mrs. Douglas smiled at him, tapping her lower lip. "Because . . ." He risked a quick glance at Max and Alex. "Because we sold it to Mrs. Douglas. For her . . . you know . . ."

Mrs. Douglas narrowed her eyes at Brian, but it was clear she was amused. "You've been yelling at these boys so much, you didn't even give them the chance to tell you that I done bought the plane already! It's on display in my little showroom in Iowa City, along with my Jet Ski, my snowmobile, my motorcycles, and my Corvette. So you don't have to worry about any more trouble from that. Besides, I'm sure you're much more interested in discussing how to get your Plastisteel operation up and running."

Dad showed the iPad to Mom. Her eyebrows went up a little. "Well, that's . . . um . . . certainly very generous of you, Mrs. Douglas." She handed back the iPad, and her eyes found Dad's. They couldn't hide their happiness. Dad even reached out and took Mom's hand.

Mrs. Douglas smiled and waved her comment away. "Oh, baby doll, that's not generous at all. For me, that's cheap! Now." She secretly winked at Brian, Max, and Alex. "Should we talk a little business?"

A short time later, the boys scrambled through the tunnel into the Eagle's Nest. Alex had stopped by his kitchen at home across the street and brought back sodas and a bag of cheese puffs.

Alex fired up Max's computer to check the *Blackbird* video online. He rubbed his knuckles under his chin. "Over ten thousand views already! If it keeps up like this, the TV and magazine people will be *begging* to tell our story."

Max frowned. "While I appreciate your single-minded devotion to profit, I still don't understand why Mrs. Douglas lied to get us out of trouble. Clearly we didn't sell *Blackbird* to her or anyone else." He looked at Alex. "Right?"

"Give me a little credit, Max. If we sold the flyer today, we'd make only a tenth of what it will be worth a few weeks from now."

"I made all that up," Brian said. "That stuff about selling *Blackbird*. I took a chance that Mrs. Douglas was on our side. She's rich and bored and just wants to have fun with her money. What's more fun than watching guys like us zip around on an experimental aircraft?"

"So our parents believe we no longer have *Blackbird*. We'll have to work on it in secret again," Max said.

"Yeah, starting with its brakes." Alex handed sodas to Brian and Max. "I can't afford to keep buying new shoes if our future landings go like our first one."

Brian took a drink of Mountain Dew. "I was thinking

we should work on her engine. You know, with some more parts, maybe we could rebuild it so *Blackbird* could take off on her own."

"But I thought we needed more Plastisteel for all that," said Alex.

"Yeah, but maybe Mrs. Douglas —"

"Could help us get more Plastisteel." Max finished Brian's sentence and laughed.

Alex sat down on a stool and looked around the Eagle's Nest. "Right back where we started."

"Not back where we started," said Brian. "Things are better now. A lot better." He looked at his two best friends standing next to *Blackbird*. "And the best is yet to come."

AUTHOR'S NOTE

I had the good fortune of living in Riverside, Iowa, for nine wonderful years. It is a nice, clean, safe town full of kind people. When I knew I wanted *Stealing Air* to be a small-town story, a story of the Midwest, set in Iowa, I knew Riverside would be the perfect place.

Although the Riverside in this novel is based on the real town of the same name, I have fictionalized many of its attributes and included different aspects of several Iowa towns I've known. The real town is smaller than the one in this novel. I've added several streets, naming some of them after streets in Dysart, Iowa, where I grew up. I also enriched Riverside by moving the beautiful town square from Washington, Iowa, seventeen miles north, and the large grain elevators from Dysart eighty miles southeast, placing the big cement towers near the English River so that Brian and Alex could fly *Blackbird* between them. The Riverside high school and junior high came back inside the city limits and gained a new mascot. I then had fun allowing the Riverside Roughriders to play the Trojans, the old mascot for the school district that used to serve Dysart. Thus, no real team's pride was hurt in the writing of this novel.

In real life and in this story, the English River does run along the south edge of Riverside, but for fictional purposes, I have significantly widened and deepened the river. I added a large railroad bridge across the river and borrowed the name "Runaway Bridge" from a railroad bridge that my friends and I used to explore when we were in fifth and sixth grade. Sadly, the real Runaway Bridge has been destroyed, but I have a piece of its limestone on my bookshelf, a reminder of that time of adventure and exploration.

Max and Brian are both fans of the classic TV show *Star Trek*, and they live in the perfect place for such fandom. Years ago, the Riverside City Council obtained permission from *Star Trek* creator Gene Roddenberry to declare Riverside the official future birthplace of Captain James T. Kirk. Now, a stone monument proclaims that the captain will be born on that site on March 22, 2228. A large model starship very like the iconic U.S.S. *Enterprise* is usually on display out by the highway. Since Riverside has this *Star Trek* tradition, I thought that Max and Brian would be just the kind of guys to share my enthusiasm for the show.

All other aspects of *Stealing Air* are purely fictional, and I hope they are fun.

If you are like Brian, Alex, Max, and me and find flying fascinating, I encourage you to check out the many photos, videos, and links to airplane websites in the *Stealing Air* section of www.trentreedy.com.

ACKNOWLEDGEMENTS

I've been periodically working on this novel for many years, and so I am indebted to many people who have helped with this story's long path to publication. Deepest thanks and heartfelt gratitude:

To all the teachers who helped shape my writing and me as a writer. To my sixth grade English teacher, Gail Gerber, for her patience with me and for assigning our class to write a story about "Freaky Frankie." To all my other teachers. Thank you for putting up with me and for making me learn in spite of my occasional resistance.

To all good teachers everywhere. You can never be thanked enough!

To those who encouraged this novel in its earliest form. To Larry and Debbie Marshall for their kindness and for saying all the right things after reading a very early version of this novel. To Melanie Harkness for an early read and for the priceless gift of her friendship.

To Jean Harmston for sending me photographs of Riverside, Iowa, that were helpful with the cover art.

To those who offered technical advice about rockets, airplanes, skateboards, and large balloons. To Jason Harkness, whose knowledge of very large and powerful model rockets is unparalleled. To Ralph Brendler for advice about the flyer's wingspan and whose mathematical skills helped me figure out the plan for the Mr. Piggly balloon. To Lee Boekelheide for taking me flying in his Cardinal and for familiarizing me with basic flight principles and airplane controls. Brian and Alex would not have flown without you!

To my family. To my brother, Tyler, for wonderful long discussions about this story and about everything else. To my sister, Tiffany, for her encouragement and inspiration, as well as for her hospitality when book business brought me to New York. To my mother, Lu Ann, for, well, being my mother, but also for buying me books and taking me to the Dysart Public Library when I was young.

To librarians everywhere! You are our greatest champions for peace, hope, and freedom.

To my Vermont College of Fine Arts family for their generous support. I am very honored to be a part of the VCFA community. The great connections I've made there are too numerous to name here, but I'm grateful for each of them. Thanks especially to my graduating class, the Cliffhangers, in particular Patti Brown, Jill Santopolo,

Carol Brendler, Carol Williams, and Marianna Baer for their help with manuscripts or other challenges in the writing life.

To the good folks at Arthur A. Levine Books and Scholastic. To Sue Flynn, Chris Satterlund, Terribeth Smith, Charles Young, and the rest of the stellar sales team. To Antonio Gonzalez, Emma Brockway, Candace Greene, Emily Clement, Paul Gagne, John Mason, Elizabeth Parisi, Lizette Serrano, and Tracy van Straaten. Thank you for all your amazing work! To Charisse Meloto, the world's greatest publicist, who brings hope and works pure magic to get the word out on my books. To Arthur Levine for a fantastic imprint. To all the other great people at Scholastic. You are incredible at what you do, and it is always an absolute pleasure to work with you.

To John and Katherine Paterson for their friendship and hospitality. To Katherine in particular for all the advice and encouragement both in the pursuit of my first publication and in helping me understand what it really means to be a writer.

To my stellar agent, Ammi-Joan Paquette, who gave me my first acceptance letter as a writer. I cherish your friendship and your spot-on advice. I'm with you all the way!

To my editor and friend, Cheryl Klein. The more I work with you, the more I believe your name also belongs on the cover of the book. Thank you for your patience with me, for working so incredibly hard, and for your brilliant ideas and guidance. You have all the best ideas about story and kidlit. I salute you.

To my wife and best friend, Amanda, with all my deepest love and admiration. You are my life.

Finally, I must especially thank readers of this book. These words are completely inadequate in expressing how grateful I am to those who have taken the time to read my work. I marvel at the thought that even in this age of infinite distraction you have chosen to spend your valuable time with a story I wrote. I can never thank you enough or repay you for your kindness, but I promise I will do my very best to continue to offer the best stories I know how to write. Thank you once again. I wish you the very best.

About the Author

Trent Reedy is the author of *Words in the Dust*, which was inspired by his experiences as a member of the National Guard in Afghanistan in 2004–2005. *Words in the Dust* was named an Al Roker's Book Club pick on the *Today Show*, an ALA Best Fiction for Young Adults selection, and to the ALA's Amelia Bloomer Project list. Born and raised in Iowa, where he taught high school English, Trent and his wife now live in Spokane, Washington. Please visit his website at www.trentreedy.com.

This book was edited by
Cheryl Klein and designed
by Christopher Stengel. The
text was set in Sabon MT.
This book was printed and
bound by R. R. Donnelley in
Crawfordsville, Indiana. The
production was supervised
by Starr Baer. The
manufacturing was
supervised by Adam Cruz.